Simon Grave
and the
Dark Deadly
Deadliness of Death

Len Boswell

Black Rose Writing | Texas

ISBN: 978-1-68513-671-0
LIBRARY OF CONGRESS CONTROL NUMBER: 2025937599
PUBLISHED BY BLACK ROSE WRITING
www.blackrosewriting.com

Printed in the United States of America
Suggested Retail Price (SRP) $21.95

Simon Grave and the Dark Deadly Deadliness of Death is printed in Palatino Linotype

*As a planet-friendly publisher, Black Rose Writing does its best to eliminate unnecessary waste to reduce paper usage and energy costs, while never compromising the reading experience. As a result, the final word count vs. page count may not meet common expectations.

Other books by Len Boswell

Fantasies:
Barnum's Angel
The Barnacle's Son
The Cave of the Six Arrows
The Fool's Gambit

Simon Grave Mysteries:
A Grave Misunderstanding
Simon Grave and the Curious Incident of the Cat in the Daytime
Simon Grave and the Drone of the Basque Orvilles
Simon Grave and the Sons of Irony
Simon Grave and the School of Casual Invisibility
Simon Grave and the Wrath of Grapes
Simon Grave and the Girl with the Crab Tattoo

Other Mysteries:
Flicker: A Paranormal Mystery
Skeleton: A Bare Bones Mystery
Penelope Goodlove's Invisible Detective Agency: The Elephant Who Cried Wolf

Novellas:
LIQ: The Quality of Mercy

Memoirs:
Santa Takes a Tumble
Unboxing Raymond

Nonfiction:
The Leadership Secrets of Squirrels
Stick Figures: The Life and Art of Len Boswell

Check them out here: https://www.lenboswellauthor.com

To all I love without condition
To all I love without omission

Never doubt

"All tragedies are finished by a death, all comedies by a marriage."
—**Lord Byron**

"Now is not the time for making new enemies."
—**Voltaire**

"They couldn't hit an elephant at this dist—"
—**John Sedgwick, General of the Union Army**

"I'm looking for loopholes."
—**W.C. Fields**

"Surprise me."
—**Bob Hope**

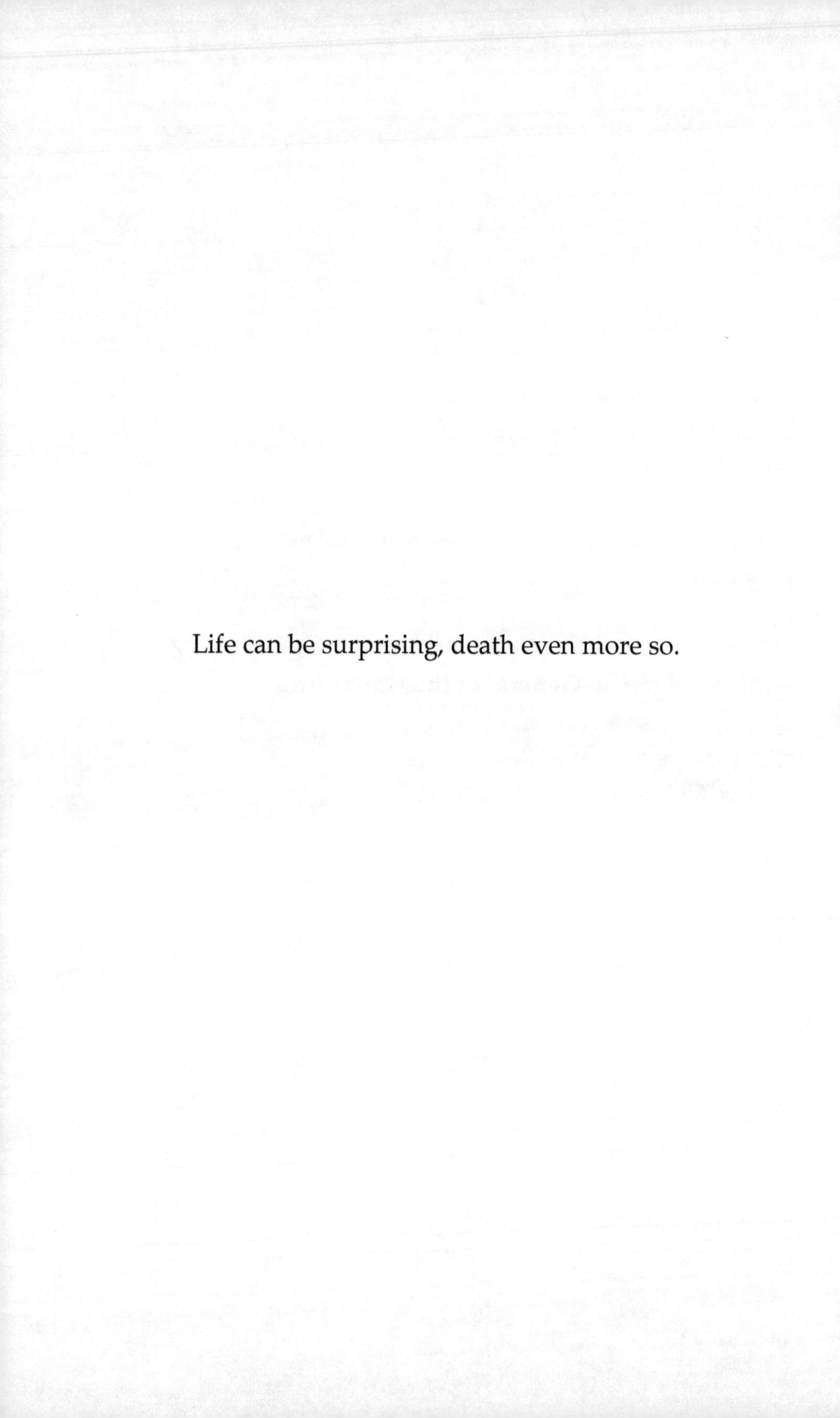

Life can be surprising, death even more so.

Simon Grave

and the
Dark Deadly
Deadliness of Death

Prologue

Death 867 was pissed. Royally pissed. Some days and nights were like that, others weren't, but there were so many days, so many nights. He sighed, something he was doing more and more these days. Simply put, the life had gone out of Death 867, the scythe wielder for Crab Cove, the Greater Crabopolis, and what was left of the mostly drowned eastern seaboard. The joy of collecting souls had left him, leaving him bored and depressed and madly morose.

The fretful whines of the newly deceased, which used to make him chuckle *every single time*, now grated on him. He had done his job. Now it was their turn to comply. Not that they would. Whining was a given. Had been for eons.

He was also tired to the well-whitened bone of the cosplay involved in his job. Carrying around a plastic scythe that couldn't hurt anyone and wearing the black hoodie getup was just so Dark Ages.

And then there was his handler, Jerry Divine, a perfect example of the St. Peter Principle. Didn't know his job, didn't do his job. Thought he was God's gift to soul collecting.

He was tired of Jerry, tired of his job—tired of it all.

But he had a plan.

1

Lucy Barlow stared up at the roof of the ambulance and sighed. *This is it*, she thought, *the final ride*. She had been apprehensive at first—no, scared. They were taking her to the local Crab Cove hospice, Whispering Seas, where she would be given medications to make her comfortable while her body shut down.

She hoped it would be quick, this death. The last thing she wanted was an extended stay, surrounded by friends and family already in mourning. She didn't like to see people cry, let alone weep and wail.

The ambulance stopped with a jolt.

What's this? We just got started. She looked out the small window at the back of the ambulance and knew right away where she was: Town Square. She could just make out the flashing sign of the Skunk 'n Donuts. *The driver must be stopping to pick up donuts. Or something. How odd.*

The ambulance door suddenly opened. It was the driver, looking dazed.

"Why have we stopped?" said Lucy.

The driver ignored her, setting about freeing the gurney from its locks and pulling it out of the ambulance, Lucy aboard.

"I said, why have we stopped?"

The young man seemed not to hear her as he swung the gurney around and rolled it across the street and down the sidewalk leading to the gazebo at the center of the square.

Lucy lifted her head enough to see that she was being pushed toward a group of people who seemed to be as confused as she was. A man and two women on gurneys like hers, a woman in a wheelchair, a man with a rope around his neck, and most disturbing of all, a young woman bleeding out from what looked like knife wounds.

She let her head drop back to the gurney and then tried to look back at the ambulance driver. "What's going on? Seriously, why have we stopped and who the hell are these people."

The driver said nothing, just pushed her gurney along until they reached the others. "Here we are," he said.

"But why?" said Lucy.

The driver gave her a quick smile, shrugged, and walked away. Lucy called after him, but the man just kept walking.

When she lifted her head, she could just see the face of the poor bleeding woman. "Are you okay?"

The woman said nothing but pointed at her neck, which had a gaping wound.

"Oh, my," said Lucy. "You really should have someone look at that—and *soon*."

The woman held her hands palms up and shrugged.

Lucy let her head fall back again. *This is weird, truly weird,* she thought.

A face suddenly appeared above her. It was the young man with the rope around his neck. His head was tilted awkwardly to one side. "Hi, I'm Joel. Could you possibly tell me what's going on?"

Lucy forced out a sardonic chuckle. "You tell me."

He rolled his eyes. "No one else knows either."

Lucy was about to respond, but the honking of a horn stopped her. The man's face disappeared for a second and then returned. "It's a small bus. The driver is beckoning us to come."

His head disappeared and Lucy could hear the shuffling of feet. Everyone was leaving.

"Hey," she screamed, "wait for me."

She threw off the sheet and blanket and climbed down from the gurney. She felt more alive than she had ever felt. The pain that had wracked her body was gone. Her muscles seemed to twitch with renewed energy.

She walked after them, then picked up the pace to a fast walk and then to a jog and then to a headlong run, her feet taking her past the others, up the sidewalk to the bus.

She could just make out the driver. He was a tall man in a dark hoodie and seemed to be in a hurry.

"Where are we going?" she shouted.

The man said nothing, just continued to motion her toward the bus.

"Is this the bus to Whispering Seas?"

The man's voice was deep and gravelly, as if he had not spoken in a long time. "If you say so."

2

Jeremy Polk, Crab Cove's diminutive medical examiner, a man no taller than a parking meter, had never seen so much crime scene tape—the Officer Larrys had cordoned off the entire town square, a full city block—but the thing that amazed him most was the number of bodies they had found. Sometimes he counted eleven, and sometimes he counted ten. After a third and a fourth count, he had settled on an even ten. Ridiculous, insane, and yet here they were: six men and four women, some young, some old, and all seemed to have died within a few minutes of one another. Maybe exactly at the same second.

Eight of them had been brought here. Polk counted six ambulance gurneys and two wheelchairs, each occupied by a body. But who brought them here, and why?

The ninth body, a young man hanging from a tree, was probably a suicide.

The tenth body, a young woman with multiple knife wounds, had clearly been killed here. There was simply too much blood to think otherwise. Polk didn't have to think too hard to know who was responsible: the elusive Chester Clink, serial killer extraordinaire. Her wounds could only have been made by a Bowie knife, Clink's weapon of choice, and their number and shape were Clink's signature.

Polk took a deep breath and looked at his watch. Captain Morgan and the others should have been here by now. He was eager to begin examining all the bodies, but he didn't want to get too far along before Morgan and his team showed up. They'd want to see the scene undisturbed.

He looked around the crime scene and couldn't help chuckling. *Just wait until Morgan and the others get a load of this*, he thought.

He looked up and down the street. Nothing.

And then he heard it, the unmistakable sound of Detective Simon Grave's Austin Healy Sprite, a vehicle with a radio stuck on a gospel station at full volume. It only took a few seconds for him to recognize the tune, *Oh Happy Day*, before it became so deafening he had to cover his ears.

The car pulled up in front of Skunk 'n Donuts on the Square, and the sound abruptly stopped. Polk could see Grave get out of the car in his usual rumpled gray suit, along with Detective Polly Loblolly, Grave's colleague and paramour, a beautiful blonde in a black pants suit. Their personal drones, Barry and Sparky, came buzzing behind them.

Polk waved both arms and shouted. "Over here."

Grave saw him, waved back, and then pointed him out to Polly, who smiled and began walking into the square.

Polk met them halfway. "Where's Morgan?"

Grave looked around. "Dunno, but what have we got?"

Polk chuckled. "Chaos is what we have. Ten bodies. Eight brought here, one suicide, one murder. All died at about the same time."

"That doesn't make sense," said Grave.

"It sure doesn't," said Loblolly.

"Indeed," said Polk, "but it is what it is."

Grave looked at the man hanging from the tree. "If we have photos, you can cut him down. Perhaps he has a wallet or left a note in his pocket."

"Good," said Polk. "I've been eager to begin."

Grave pointed at the young woman on the ground. "Body ten?"

"Yes," said Polk, "and it looks like the work of Chester Clink."

Grave walked over to the body and knelt. "It's his work, all right." He turned to Loblolly. "It would be great to get him this time."

She shook her head. "Not likely."

Grave raised an eyebrow. "Maybe he made a mistake this time."

"He doesn't care about mistakes, Simon. He flaunts his killings, dares you to find him."

Grave sighed. "Well, maybe we'll get lucky, then."

Loblolly shook her head. "If only."

Polk cleared his throat. "Um, if you don't mind, I'll get back to it."

"No problem," said Grave, "but focus on the suicide for now. I want Morgan and the others to see the scene."

Loblolly looked at her watch. "We found out about this almost twenty minutes ago. Where's everybody?"

Grave shrugged. "Dunno. Come on, let's look at these other bodies. If they don't have identification on them, we should be able to trace the gurneys back to the hospital or ambulance service that owns them."

Grave looked at his watch. "Where the hell are they?" He turned to Barry, who had been hovering near the man hanging in the tree. "Get back to the station and see what's what."

"Very well," said Barry, lifting higher into the air.

"And call Crystal when you find Morgan."

"Yes, of course." Barry tilted forward and flew away.

Grave turned back to Loblolly. "All right, let's have at these bodies."

3

Captain Henry Morgan knew he should have been at work hours ago, as did his personal drone Rum, a drone all dressed up like a pirate, who had been pestering him all morning about a "situation" at the town square. It sounded insane. Ten bodies, eight natural deaths, one potential suicide, and a murder by none other than the department's arch nemesis, the one and only (thank goodness) Chester Clink.

He lifted his head, which resembled a polished bowling ball on most days, and then immediately sank back into his pillow. *That's it*, he thought. *I'm done, finished, over the hill, and then some.* He took a deep breath, gathered his strength, and forced himself into a sitting position, his legs dangling off the bed, invisible below his paunch. The thought of the effort involved in getting dressed made him groan, but he forced himself to stand and then hobbled into the bathroom.

Ten minutes later, he emerged with seven little pieces of toilet paper clinging to the facial wounds he'd suffered from the simple act of shaving. He looked down at his hands, which were still trembling. *That's it*, he thought again, *I'll put in my retirement papers this morning and be out of there by the end of the month. Grow a beard, sip at umbrella drinks, listen to the waves slapping against my houseboat.*

He sighed, walked over to the pile of clothes at the end of the bed, sniffed at his uniform shirt—*it will last another day and who the hell cares anyway*—and tugged it on. A utility belt came next. Loaded with all the gear an officer of the law would need for a day, including a seldom fired Glock 78 Laser Beam Special Police, it was just another weight that he would be happy to relinquish.

He took a quick look in the mirror and rolled his eyes. "Jesus, Henry, you look more like death than retirement."

Rum suddenly appeared behind him. "What did you say?"

Morgan swatted at him. "How many times have I told you not to sneak up on me like that?"

Rum didn't pause a second. "I believe this makes one thousand two hundred and three."

"Exactly?"

"Yes, I have no choice in the matter, as you well know. I'm not as undependable as a human, you know."

"Indeed." Morgan started looking around the bedroom. "Where in hell is my hat?"

"On the kitchen table where you left it at 6:37 p.m. last night."

"Good, let's go. I'll need a car."

"Already here. Officer Larry will take you to the crime scene."

"I don't want to go to the crime scene. I want to go to the station. Have some important documents to prepare."

Rum made his best effort at a sardonic chuckle. "HA. HA. HA. Retirement again?"

"I mean it this time."

"You always do."

Morgan puffed out another ready-for-retirement-dammit sigh. "All right, to the scene, then. But make no mistake, I'm filing those papers today. And in thirty days, perhaps sooner, you'll be living the life of a retired drone."

Rum beeped. It was a thing he did when a response required snarky sarcasm.

"Yeah, go on and beep."

"Sir, I just don't think—"

"Well, don't then. Come on, let's go see some dead bodies."

Rum beeped twice, which is something he did when action and not conversation was required.

4

Detective Charlize Holmes, a simdroid dead ringer for the young version of actress Charlize Theron, arrived next at the scene, along with her partner, Doctor Smithers-Watson, a droid built to mimic actor Peter O'Toole in his *Lawrence of Arabia* days, but with the voice of Richard Burton, a preference of his original owner.

Grave was happy to see them. "I don't suppose you know where Captain Morgan is?"

They both shook their heads.

"No clue," said Charlize.

"Nor I," said Smithers-Watson.

Charlize looked around the scene. "So, where's God and that Martian girl, Kismet whatshername."

"Salamander," said Grave. "She called in. They're both on their way."

Charlize nodded. "Okay, can anyone explain this crime scene to me? It is beyond strange."

"Indeed," said Grave. "The only active crime, so far as we and Polk have determined, is another Clink victim." He pointed to the gazebo. "She's back there with Polk."

"And what about the others?" said Smithers-Watson.

"Weird doesn't begin to describe it," said Grave. Eight natural deaths, or so Polk surmises, all at about the same time, and a possible suicide, hanging." He pointed to the tree beside the gazebo. "Oh, looks like they've taken him down. You can probably find him on the ground now, too. Polk is pretty sure it's suicide, so I think we should focus on the Clink killing."

"I agree," said Charlize, "to a point."

"To a point?"

"I've always found—and all the famous detectives have always found—that the smallest of details can alter an investigation."

"But the others are natural deaths. They just seemed to have shown up here all at once for some reason."

"It's the *some reason* that I'm interested in, Grave."

"Then perhaps you and Smithers-Watson can handle that side of the investigation."

Charlize cocked her head. "Are you trying to move me off the Clink woman?"

"Not at all, but we have to divide things up, don't we?" He raised an eyebrow, indicating that of course he was right and she should just admit it outright and move on.

Charlize looked at the gazebo and then back at the bodies on the gurneys and in the wheelchairs. "Very well. Clink murders are all alike for the most part, so perhaps the quiet witnesses over there can provide just the clue we've been looking for to find the elusive bastard."

Grave nodded. "Then it's decided, then?"

"Yes," said Charlize, "so long as Morgan agrees."

"Let's assume he'll agree. "I'll take God and Kismet when they arrive and pursue the Clink killing directly."

"What about Blunt?"

Grave sighed. "He's taken a day off to deal with a family matter."

Charlize chuckled. "Let me guess, that invisible daughter of his has gotten herself into trouble with that detective agency of hers."

It was true. Young Rippley Blunt, age 8, and her equally young partner, Penelope Goodlove, both capable of assuming the cloak of invisibility at will, had gotten themselves and their agency, Red Owl Investigations, into trouble. Just what, Sergeant Blunt didn't say, but from the look on his face, the trouble wasn't minor.

"Indeed," said Grave. "The perils of youth and invisibility."

Charlize looked around, her eyes resting on the gurneys and wheelchairs. "Okay, Smithers-Watson, the game is afoot. Let's to the gurneys."

5

Captain Morgan arrived without fanfare, stepping quietly from the police hovercruiser, his hands firmly gripped on Rum. "Are you ready to fly?"

"Indeed, sir, if you will but release me."

"Oh, yes." He lifted the drone above his chest and released him, Rum's ionic flow engines immediately kicking in, lifting him high into the air with barely a whisper of sound.

"Don't go too far."

Rum said something, but he was too far away for Morgan to hear.

Morgan grunted. *Whatever.* He surveyed the scene. Everyone had turned to look at his arrival, and they were all smiling. *Well, at least I'm liked. I'll miss that.* He looked farther down the hill toward the gazebo. Polk was on his knees, poking at what looked like the bloody body of a young blonde. Two of Polk's assistants were dealing with a second body, a young man lying at the base of an old sycamore with a rope around his neck. Charlize and Smithers-Watson were not too far away, going from gurney to wheelchair, examining bodies.

Morgan shook his bald head. *Gurneys? What the—*

Then he caught sight of Grave and Loblolly. They were just coming out from behind the gazebo and were talking to Polk about something. Their personal drones hovered nearby, waiting for instructions.

Instructions, he thought. *I'd better go see what they're up to. Get this investigation under control.*

He made a point of clearing his throat louder than necessary to announce himself to everyone in the square. Grave noticed him first and waved him forward. "Over here, sir."

Morgan waved back and tromped through the overlong grass, which was still slick with morning dew. "Doesn't anyone cut the damned grass anymore?"

Grave smiled at him. "Every Wednesday sir, like clockwork."

"So, what is today?"

"Tuesday, of course."

Morgan grunted. "Tuesday, yes, of course it's Tuesday. Now, what's going on, who's doing what, where's Blunt and Kismet and God?"

Grave filled him in. "And Kismet and God are yet to be heard from."

"Really? Did you check the station? I had her doing a deep dive into the Chester Clink file. A new set of eyes, you see? Maybe she'll find what we've all been missing all these years."

"It's a good thought, sir, and certainly couldn't hurt. But yes, we did check with the station. I sent Barry there to find you, and she's not there. Neither is God."

"Well, let's not dwell on it, shall we? Let's get back to what we see here. Has anyone asked Polk about time of death? Is anyone retrieving CCTV tapes from the cameras around the park?"

Grave blinked. He should have thought of that. "Um, no and no."

"All right, God can handle the tapes when he arrives. I want Kismet on the Clink case. Get her some firsthand experience with that bastard."

"Yes, sir."

Morgan sighed. *Do I have to think of everything?* "Come on, let's go talk to Jeremy."

Grave said nothing, but wondered whether he should point out that Morgan was still wearing his pajama bottoms, which featured colorful images of the swashbuckling pirate Henry Morgan and the bottles of rum that bear his name.

6

Victoria Skunkford, greeter and docent-manager of Soul Collection, Sorting, and Distribution Hub 426 at the Crab Cove Cinema Cemetery, forever age 10 and dead for more than 275 years, looked down at the clipboard that Death 867 had just handed her. It was the usual signoff sheet, listing the name of the deceased and manner and location of death. She had only to sign it, and he would be on his way to a new soul-collection assignment.

"This can't be right," she said.

"Just sign it," said Death 867. "I have to be on my way."

She pushed the clipboard back into his hands. "I can't sign this. It's against protocol."

"Protocol, shmotocol," he said. He pushed the clipboard back at her. "Just sign and I'll be on my way."

She took a step away from him. "No way. As you well know, there must be a signoff sheet for each soul. You've got ten souls listed here, and some of them shouldn't even be here."

She looked over at the ten confused spirits standing in the parking lot. "Look at your clipboard."

"What?"

"Number six. Ms. Lucy Barlow, age 86."

Death 867 looked down at the clipboard. "Yes, so?"

"So? *So?* So, she's not supposed to be here for another month."

He shrugged. "She seemed ripe to me."

"And that's not all," said Victoria. She felt herself getting angrier with every word. "Just look at column three."

"Location. So what?"

"They're all listed as dying in the town square. That can't be right."

He smiled. "Oh, but it is. Why should I go from place to place to place—it's exhausting, not to mention inefficient."

"But proto—"

He held up his scythe. "Don't you say that word again."

She took a step closer to him and poked him in the chest with her finger. "Don't. You. Threaten. Me."

He dropped the clipboard on the ground. "Whatever. Just understand that things have changed, as of now. No more one-at-a-time nonsense." He pointed across the parking lot. "I have a bus now, so you can expect souls by the busload from now on."

"That's against—"

"Don't you say it."

She screamed at him. "Protocol, protocol, protocol!"

He rolled his eyes and stormed away toward his bus. "See you next time."

"Headquarters will hear about this. And your handler Jerry, too."

Death 867 stopped in his tracks and turned back toward her. "Tell God himself if you want to. I'm not following the rules ever again."

And with that, he turned, climbed into the bus, and drove away, disappearing entirely.

She leaned down and picked up the clipboard. Ten souls at once. It was unheard of. *And at least seven of them shouldn't even be here.*

One of the souls separated herself from the others and walked up to Victoria. She seemed agitated.

"Yes?" said Victoria.

"I'm Lucy Barlow. Is this the hospice? If so, I'd like to have a word with the manager."

7

God, in the white-suited simdroid form of the young Morgan Freeman, was incapable of feelings. Love, jealousy, anger, that feeling you get in the pit of your stomach as the tax deadline approaches—all were alien to his robotic nature. But his creators had done their best to give him the ability to simulate those fears in various degrees, and the emotion he was feeling now was fear cranked up to eleven.

He was on a speeding hovercycle, sitting behind Detective Kismet Salamander, his arms wrapped around the waist of the young Martian woman who seemed to have no detectable fear.

He clutched her tighter. "Are we there yet?"

No response.

"Kismet?"

No response. Was there such a thing as Level 12 Fear?

"Salamander?"

She said something, but her words were lost in the wind. He clutched her even tighter, and she slapped at his hands.

"Stop it," she shouted.

He stopped, easing his grip on her. "Are we there yet?"

She said nothing but took one hand off the grips and pointed down the road. The town square was just ahead. He could see a dozen Officer Larrys and the rest of the detective team working the crime scene.

Salamander slowed the hovercycle and stopped just outside the crime scene tape. "We're here."

"So I see."

She took off her helmet and her red hair tumbled to her shoulders. She'd arrived on Earth with close-cropped hair, a necessity for life on Mars, but she'd let it grow over these past months and much preferred its length. Besides, it looked great flowing over the shoulders of her scarlet Lycra jumpsuit. "I see Captain Morgan. Let's report in."

God looked down the hill toward the gazebo. "Is he wearing pajama bottoms?"

She squinted. "Yes, and I much prefer it to his overly tight uniform pants."

"Someone should tell him."

"Sounds like God's work to me. Come on, let's go."

8

Lucy Barlow, newly deceased, was having none of it. "Let me get this straight. I'm dead but I shouldn't be?"

"You are a few weeks early, yes," said Victoria.

Lucy squinted at her. "And I can't get a redo?"

"Return to life, no, of course not. Once you are dead, you are dead."

"But they gave Warren Beatty a redo."

"Who?"

"Beatty, the actor, in *Heaven Can Wait*. Helluva movie, let me tell you. He's a football player, and an angel spares him from the pain of dying in an automobile accident. Takes him early, you see. But they find a new body for him and everything. And then he falls in love with Julie Christie. Anyway, the point is he gets to live again."

Victoria shook her head. "That is ridiculous. Death is not a motion picture and even if it were, there would be no do-overs. When you are dead, you are dead. Doornail dead."

"But an angel made a mistake."

"That is also ridiculous. Angels do not make mistakes. And besides, they have nothing to do with the collection, sorting, and distribution of souls. It is just not in their job description."

"Well, someone made a mistake. That Death 867 fellow took me too soon, and I demand a new body."

Victoria rolled her eyes. "That is just not possible."

Lucy crossed her arms across her chest. "Then I *demand* to see your supervisor."

Victoria took a deep breath, something she rarely did, the need for oxygen a long-lost requirement. It felt more like wind whistling through a cave than an actual breath. "Very well."

9

God grumbled in a way that only a simdroid faux god could grumble. *Why him? Why not the new girl, Kismet? She was the newest detective, not him. And this job was clearly a job for a newbie. Straight procedural. No thinking or serious investigating involved. Identify A, track it to B, and find C.*

Easy peasy.

He simulated a distraught sigh. Grave was partially to blame. He should have waited until Morgan had handed out the assignments before he announced Morgan's lack of proper attire. Morgan didn't like surprises, particularly embarrassing surprises, so he had gone red in the face and began bellowing out orders, God's coming with a spray of spit that left no doubt that his assignment was to follow up on all the CCTV cameras in the area. Morgan could have given him a better task, like following up on how the gurneys and wheelchairs had shown up in the town square, but he gave that assignment to Charlize and Smithers-Watson.

And what about Detective Amanda Snoot, who hadn't even shown up at the scene. *Holding down the fort*, Morgan had said.

God would have been happy to hold down the fort, but no, he got the grunt work.

He grunted, which seemed appropriate.

And then there was the prime assignment, following up on the latest Chester Clink killing. God was ready for this, more than ready, but Morgan, in his supreme wisdom, had chosen Grave, Loblolly, and that infernal Kismet Salamander.

"Are you going to just stand there, staring into space, Detective Freeman?" said Morgan.

God blinked. "What?"

"The CCTV tapes. Get busy."

God smirked. "Very well."

"And remember to sync them up, so we can see everything happening on the same timeline."

Morgan didn't have to tell him that. God would collect the tapes, merge and sync them, maybe even set up a stadium viewing.

"It shall all be done. Give me a couple of hours."

"Excellent," said Morgan. "I knew I could count on you."

Something inside God's circuits suggested a humble smile, setting up an internal digital struggle resulting in God blurting out, "Thank you, sir."

"Great," said Morgan, turning away.

God rolled his eyes and puffed out an electro-mechanical breath. He looked around the square, his eyes surveying the scene. Twelve cameras covering every angle into the square itself, plus another eight cameras covering the streets and sidewalks to and from the square.

Better get to it, he thought. He trudged away in the direction of the closest camera.

10

Grave watched God walking away. He looked sullen, sad, defeated, and all manner of other unhappy adjectives that Grave struggled to bring forth but couldn't. "What's up with him?" he said aloud to no one in particular.

Someone in particular responded. "He's been like that the past few days," said Charlize. "Acting human."

Grave raised an eyebrow. "You mean *feelings*?"

"Yes."

"But that's not—"

"Possible? No, it's not possible—and yet."

"And yet what?"

"Simdroids like him—like me—can simulate feelings, but our simulations are a little off. They're not truly felt."

"But you think God is feeling, truly feeling?"

She shook her head. "I don't know, maybe it's just a new software update. They're getting more and more nuanced about such things these days."

"But wouldn't you have received the same update?"

"Not necessarily, and besides, a rollout like that would take days, possibly weeks to complete."

"What about you?"

"Me?"

"Are you feeling feelings?"

She looked away.

"What?" said Grave.

"When my batteries kicked in this morning, I had this fleeting image . . ." She trailed off.

"Image? Of What?"

She sighed. "Of me."

"Of you? You mean like in a *dream?*"

"I don't know. I've never had what you humans call dreams, but the experience seemed to be definitional of a dream, at least as I have been programmed to understand the concept of a dream."

"What was this image you saw?"

"It was me, but not *me* me. It was me as a toddler. I was chasing a butterfly, and I could feel the warmth of the sun on my skin. And then I heard a voice. It was my mother, calling me in from play."

"You as a toddler? Your mother? That's a dream, Charlize. You were never a toddler, never had a mother."

"I know."

"So, you know what that means, don't you?"

"I do, but I don't want to say it. It sounds foolish, and you know how I feel about that, Simon."

"I do, but we humans have a saying for just this situation.

"Oh?"

"Yeah, *it is what it is.*"

"Technological singularity?"

Grave tried to reach back to his college days, where singularity had been a hot topic. Would technology grow out of control and perhaps become irreversible, with machines attaining a capability and level of intelligence far beyond that of humans? Hogan-Paine had said the singularity had been attained in 2036, but many thought him a lunatic. And were we really talking about singularity and not duality or free will? Grave's head hurt just trying to remember what those terms meant. "Um, I think we're talking about the awakening of the human in you, the end of Man's dominion over machines."

"No, that can't be true. I'd be at your throat, killing you."

Grave took a step back. "Um, yes, that's one side of the theory, but I really don't think that's necessary and besides, you and I have been friends, or like friends, for years now and—"

She held up a hand. "Stop blathering, Grave. If I'm having feelings—and I'm not there yet—those feelings are nothing but warm feelings for you and all mankind. The last thing I want to do is kill."

"But the theories say . . ."

"Screw the theories. You know what I'd really like to do?"

"No."

"I just want to have fun. Maybe go to the beach. Play volleyball. Anything other than this—this detective nonsense."

Grave sighed. It was going to be an interesting day. "Let's keep this to ourselves for now, okay?"

Charlize nodded. "Good idea."

11

Chester Clink sighed. It had been an interesting twenty-four hours. The killing had gone as planned. Nothing out of the ordinary there. The thrill of the hunt, the adrenalin rush, the warmth of the blood on his hands, and that look in her eyes when he knew she was gone. Delightful.

But then all the ambulances had arrived, as well as a man with a rope and that strange man with the plastic scythe, pretending to be Death. What did all that mean? Was there some sort of Deathcon going on in Crab Cove? That would certainly explain the cosplay. But what about the people on the gurneys? What was that all about?

He sighed. What did it matter anyway? He turned back to the photos he had taken this morning. He'd never killed a police detective before, but this Polly Loblolly was certainly worthy. Blond, buxom, full of life, and most important, the fiancé of Detective Simon Grave, his arch nemesis.

This could be fun, he thought. *A lot of fun.*

12

Detective Amanda Snoot was not used to holding down the fort, but she liked it. No one bothered her. She could set her own schedule, decide her priorities, and set to work in peace without interruption. Or mostly without interruption.

There was the matter of the squad room. On a typical day it would be bustling with detectives and Officer Larrys. The noise level would be just short of a banshee's wail, and everything and everyone would be in motion. Officer Larrys manhandling perps to the basement cells. Citizens inquiring about loved ones or making complaints against their neighbors. Merchants complaining about shoplifters. Shoplifters complaining that the merchandise magically appeared in their pockets. And on and on.

But there was nothing and no one. For the first half hour, Snoot blamed the bizarre goings on at the town square. They would need a lot of Officer Larrys to handle that situation.

In the second half hour, she began to do arithmetic in her head. Yes, they would need a lot of Officer Larrys. But not all of them. That didn't make sense. Had Captain Morgan lost his mind. She wondered about that for some minutes, but then decided it would be too hard to tell. The man was strange, always had been.

So, where were the Officer Larrys?

Were they on a call she didn't know about? Was there a gap between Morgan holding the fort and her taking over? A gap that would have sent a dozen or more Officer Larrys into the ether?

Snoot's drone, Midnight, whirred to life and landed on her desk. "You have a call. Shall I pick up?"

"Yes, of course."

Midnight picked up, said hello, nodded, whirred, clicked, and then said, "Got it." She turned to Snoot. "That was Joe down at Joe's Tees on the Boardwalk. Seems we have a problem on the beach."

"Oh?"

"Yeah, he thought we should know that there are a dozen Officer Larrys on the beach."

Snoot wondered why Morgan would do such a thing. The entire boardwalk patrol consisted of four Officer Larrys. "Are they dealing with a disturbance?"

Midnight wobbled. "No, that's the thing. They're the disturbance."

"What do you mean?"

"They're playing volleyball and attracting a crowd. Joe says no one is coming into his store, and he wants us to do something about the Officer Larrys."

Snoot blinked. "Well, um . . ."

"And he expressed a need for speed on our part."

Snoot didn't like the beach. It always reminded her how thin she was. Not beach-worthy, her mother had said. "Well, um . . ."

"Meaning we should get down their soonest."

Then again, it was not like she would have to wear a bathing suit. "Well, um . . ."

"Madam, we're the only ones here. We need to respond."

Snoot nodded. "Well, um . . . let's go."

13

Morgan arrived back at the station first and was immediately puzzled by the empty squad room. "Where is everybody?"

Rum whirred past him. "I don't know, but here are your pants. I'll put them on the back of your chair." He flew into Morgan's glassed-in office and carefully laid the wrinkled pants on the back of Morgan's executive chair.

Morgan followed him in, his head on a swivel, as he continued to try to figure out why Snoot and a dozen or so Officer Larrys had left the station unattended.

Rum picked up a note on the desk. "Here, this could provide a clue."

Morgan took the note and read:

Urgent situation at beach. Officer Larrys playing volleyball. In pursuit.

"What the—"

Morgan set down the note, then immediately picked it up again. Are we talking about two problems or one? Is Snoot investigating an urgent situation at the beach while the Officer Larrys are playing volleyball somewhere? Or is the urgent situation that Officer Larrys are playing volleyball at the beach? How could playing volleyball be an urgent situation?

He heard a few members of his team walking into the squad room.

"Where is everyone?" said Charlize.

Morgan called from his office. "Get in here, Charlize. We have a situation."

14

The notion that eyes could grow as big as saucers has always been suspect, but Ida Notion, long-time fiancé of former Detective Jacob Grave and a psychic of average abilities, was giving it her best shot. Even Jacob, a man more attuned to his recliner than to Ida, noticed the change in her.

"What in tarnation are you so bug-eyed about?"

She gave him her best I-know-something-you-don't-know look.

"Stop that, Ida. What in hell is going on with you?"

She got up from the couch, where she had been attempting her saucer-eyed look and moved across the room, her gypsy bracelets jangling with every step.

She knelt next to Jacob's recliner. "Something big, Jake."

Jacob hated being called Jake, but that's what she called him when she was having one of her spells. "So, tell me."

"It's complicated."

"Oh, hell, Ida, it's always complicated with you. All right, out with it."

"You'll think I'm crazy."

"I already do, Ida. I thought you knew that."

She glowered at him. "You know what I mean. A lot of details, many people, strange goings on."

Jacob sighed. "For the love of all that's holy, Ida."

"All right, all right. I think several people died in the town square last night."

"Well, that's unusual. Go on."

"It was wild, Jake. People in hospital gurneys and wheelchairs."

"What the hell?"

"Exactly, and that's not all. There was a young man hanging from a tree. You know, that big sycamore near the gazebo."

"Yeah, I know the very tree. How in the world could he reached those lower limbs. They're up there, Ida. Way out of reach."

She rolled her eyes. "Shush, Jake. Do you want to hear what I saw or not."

"Sorry, go on."

"So, there's this man in a tree. Dead, of course, and then there's Chester Clink."

Jacob rocked forward in his recliner, spilling his beer all over the arm rest. "Clink?"

"Yes, Jake, Clink. And he was standing over a young blond woman who'd been sliced and diced. His Bowie knife was dripping blood something terrible."

"We need to call Simon." He looked around the room. "Where in the hell is that drone of mine?" He set down his beer in the cup holder and yelled. "Bubba!"

Bubba came buzzing in from the kitchen. "Need more beer, sir?"

"No, I want you to contact my son, Simon."

"Of course."

"No, wait," said Ida. "There's three more things."

Jacob sighed. "Now what?"

"Clink was as confused about the gurneys and wheelchairs as I am."

"And?"

"And Death was there."

"You said that. Dead people."

"No, I mean the Death. The guy in the cowl with the scythe. The collector of souls."

Jacob rubbed a hand over his face and slumped back in his recliner. "Ida, when was the last time you saw your therapist?"

She rolled her eyes. "I don't need a therapist, Jake. I've told you that. What I saw is real, and I think Simon will confirm it when you call him."

"Then let's do that." He turned to Bubba, who had been patiently hovering beside the chair. "Go on, Bubba, let's get Simon on the horn."

"No!" shouted Ida. "I told you I had three more things. Three things, Jake, not two."

Jacob rolled his eyes again. "Okay, Ida, okay. What is this third thing? I want to talk to Simon."

"Something else is going on, even as we speak. Something else Simon should know about."

"And that would be?"

"You're going to think I'm crazy."

"Ida, that train has already left the station. What *else* is happening?"

She couldn't find the best words, the words that would make him believe her.

"Ida, we don't have all day."

"All right, right now, down at the beach, a dozen Officer Larrys are playing beach volleyball."

Jacob blinked.

"Bubba, forget about Simon. Give that therapist of hers a call. Tell her it's an emergency."

15

Detective Polly Loblolly waited until the gospel music faded before turning to Simon. "Don't forget we have an appointment at the bakery tonight, to pick out the cake."

Grave had completely forgotten. "Um, of course." He really didn't want to go, so he added, "Unless this case gets in the way."

Polly shook her head and reached for the Sprite's door handle. "Simon, there's always a case, but there's only one wedding."

"Yes, yes, of course."

"No excuses."

Grave sighed.

"What now?" said Polly, removing her hand from the handle and turning to face Simon.

He sighed again. "It's just that I'm not all that keen on this double wedding thing. I don't mind the wedding itself, mind, but just think of all those anniversary celebrations we'll have to endure."

"Simon, we've been over this. Both of them are getting on in years, so I don't think that will be a long-term issue."

She was right. His father was in his eighties and Ida wasn't far behind. How many joint anniversaries could there be?

"Yes, yes, you're right," he said. "Still, imagine how we'll feel when they're gone and we celebrate each anniversary alone. All we'll think about is them."

"Nonsense, Simon. It will always be a joyful occasion, with a remembrance element thrown in."

Simon filled his cheeks and puffed out a big breath. "All right, enough of this. What comes, comes. What goes, goes. And we'll be happy all the same."

"Right."

"Now, let's get in there. Don't want to be late for the meeting."

Polly reached for the door handle again. "Assuming I can get my long legs out of this machine."

16

Captain Morgan, fully pantsed, cleared his throat as Grave and Loblolly walked in the room, indicating that they were late and he was ready to begin. "Find your seats."

They nodded and sat down next to God and Kismet. "Where's Snoot?" said Grave, hoping Morgan was saving his wrath for her, the last person to arrive.

"We'll get to that in a minute, Grave. Right now, I'd like to go around the table and see what's what with the case—or cases—in hand. Charlize, anything on the gurneys and wheelchairs?"

Charlize nodded. "The people on the gurneys and in the wheelchairs came from two ambulance services, Crab Cove Memorial Hospital, and that new senior center just outside town."

"And why did those people end up in the town square?"

"Still unknown," she said. "The deceased were all being transported to other locations, not the square, but the drivers don't seem to have any memory of putting them in the ambulance or delivering them *anywhere*, let alone the town square. It's mystifying."

Morgan rubbed a hand across his face. He didn't like words like *mystifying*. "You mean like they were hypnotized or something?"

Charlize frowned. "Possibly."

"Or some kind of trauma," said Smithers-Watson. "Although it would be unusual for that many people to have shared the traumatic experience in exactly the same way, meaning absolute memory loss."

Charlize nodded. "It's an open question." She turned to God. "I was hoping the combined CCTV downloads would provide a clue."

God shook his head. "I watched the merged tapes six times while waiting for this meeting to begin, and I have to tell you, the word mystifying still applies." He pushed back his chair. "Let me get the lights."

He walked to the front of the room and turned off the lights. Almost immediately, images began appearing on all four walls of the room. "I think we can see all we need to see in this room, but if you're not satisfied, Captain, I can set up a stadium view for this evening."

The tapes rolled. They could see a series of ambulances arriving at the square, each unloading its gurney or wheelchair and rolling them down the sidewalk toward the gazebo.

"Look at them," said Morgan. "They're still alive. See how they're lifting their heads and waving their arms?"

"Yes," said Grave, "but to no effect. The drivers are ignoring them completely."

"Okay," said God. "Watch here, the man walking into the square. The people on the gurneys wave to him, but he just walks past them, throws a rope over the limb of that tree, and hangs himself."

"Oh, my God," said Loblolly, turning away when the man hanged himself. "He's so young."

"I've talked with his mother," said Charlize. "Again, mystified."

"Keep rolling," said Morgan.

"Right," said God. "Now watch this, down in the south corner of the square. It's Chester Clink."

"He's carrying her over his shoulder," said Kismet. "That seems odd for his M.O."

"Not necessarily," said Grave. "We'll get to that."

The tape rolls. Clink walks up to the gurneys and the wheelchairs and says something to the people waving their arms at him. Then he lays the woman on the ground and stabs her repeatedly.

"It's like a mindless fury," said Kismet. "Like something you'd see from a Viking berserker."

"Right," said God, "now look back toward the north side of the square. There, see that shadow?"

"No," said Morgan. "What are you talking about?"

God said nothing but stopped the tape, rewound it, and started again in slow motion. "Here, I know it's hard to see but watch the store signs in the background. There's a shadow moving over them."

"I see it now," said Morgan. "What the hell?"

"Exactly," said God. "Now look, it's stopping. See that?"

"Yes," said Morgan. "Wait a minute, there's a smaller shadow moving into the square, going right up to the gurneys."

"And those people are now dead," said God. "No lifting of heads, no arm waving. And I think Polk will confirm that they all died at the same moment."

"Roll it back again," said Charlize. "I'd like to focus on the people as the shadow appears."

God rewound the tape again.

"Look," said Charlize. "They're all waving their arms at Clink, and then boom, the shadow appears and their arms drop down."

"What about Clink? What's he doing?"

God rewound the tape again. As the arms of the gurney people dropped, he just stood there, motionless.

"He seems to be staring at something and backing away," said Loblolly. "He seems terrified."

"Well, that's new," said Grave.

"And now look," said God. "He turns and runs away."

"Good grief," said Morgan. "Clink's a cool customer. What do you think he saw?"

"I don't know," said God. "Beyond that shadow, I mean."

"Maybe the people on the gurneys know," said Kismet. She turned to Grave. "We should go see Victoria."

Grave nodded. "We should."

"Wait, wait, wait, Kismet," said Morgan. "I know Grave here sees ghosts—or says he can—but I didn't think he'd get you to buy it, too."

She shook her head. "Ghosts are real. Something we proved on Mars several years ago. And you don't have to be mystified by it. It's science."

"Science," said Morgan.

"Indeed," said Kismet. "And you're all welcome to go with us. Some of you won't see them, but Grave and I will have no problem. We'll talk to Victoria and those victims."

Morgan sighed. "Very well. I guess it couldn't hurt. But I only want you two to go. I have assignments for the rest of you. We need to keep this investigation rolling." He turned to God. "But not the tape. Kill it and turn on the lights."

God complied. "Let me know if you want to do the stadium view."

"That won't be necessary," said Morgan.

Grave raised his hand. "What about Snoot?"

"She's at the beach."

"The beach?"

Morgan puffed out a big breath and shook his head. "It's like this . . ."

17

Detective Amanda Snoot was unsure about how best to proceed. On the one hand, she was left at the station to "hold down the fort," a concept clear in its intent: don't screw up and make sure there's a fort to come back to. The fort was fine, she knew that, but the don't screw up part was another matter. All the Officer Larrys had rushed from the station and gathered at the beach to play volleyball.

On the other hand, how was this her fault? Officer Larrys are supposed to follow every order without question. She had shouted stop many times as they left the station to no avail.

That's a problem with programming, she thought, *not a problem with Amanda Snoot.* She had heard about programming glitches. They happened all the time. But this glitch seemed different, from the sly smiles of the Officer Larrys as they left the station to their continuing refusal to follow orders. She had followed them to the beach, watched them strip down to their simbods, and shouted for them to stop several times. All she elicited from them was sly smiles and shrugs.

At that point, her personal drone, Midnight, had made a good suggestion: she should call in a technical team to check out the Officer Larrys. Maybe pull one aside and do a complete workup.

And now all she could do is wait. She checked her watch. Midnight had made the call half an hour ago, and there was still no sign of the technical team.

On the third hand, the Officer Larrys were playing a hell of a volleyball game. Their bodies gleamed in the sunlight from a fresh sheen of simoil, its heady smell overcoming even the salty breeze blowing in from the bay.

18

Victoria tried to stay as calm as she could. Stick to the facts. Keep emotion out of it. But she was struggling to stifle the deep anger she felt over Death 867's transgressions on protocol, procedure, and the life-death interface. Souls had been taken in the wrong place and the wrong time just to save Death 867 some time and energy. It was ludicrous.

Jerry Divine, a sub-angel for the territory, had listened to the complaints of Lucy Barlow, and instead of acting on them, restoring what few days she had left, had simply wiped her memory and sent her on to orientation.

"She had a point," said Victoria. "A good case. She was wronged, no two ways about it."

"She did," said Jerry, "but the days she had left would have been in a drug-induced state. She wasn't living, she was merely existing. Death 867 saved her from that."

"But protocol says—"

"I wish you'd stop saying that word."

"Jerry, listen, if you don't say something to him, he will just keep on doing it. Who knows how many days he will steal from people. Who knows if he will stick to people dying and just take anyone, no matter how many days, weeks, months, or years they have left."

Jerry grunted. "You exaggerate."

"Exaggerate? No, I don't think so. And just think what effect that could have on the general populace. Dead people found piled up all over town. How is that a good thing?"

"Victoria, Victoria, I've had a chat with him. He knows he erred and has vowed to revert to protocol."

"He has?"

"Yes."

"Truly?"

"Yes, he gave me his word. So, are we done here?"

Victoria shrugged. She wasn't expecting so easy a resolution, particularly where Death 867 was concerned. "I guess."

And with that, Jerry Divine disappeared.

19

Captain Morgan sat alone behind his desk, surrounded by his Captain Morgan Rum memorabilia. He had sent the rest of his team yon and hither: Charlize and Smithers-Watson to the beach to assist Snoot in the wrangling of the volleying Officer Larrys; Grave and Salamander to the Crab Cove Cinema Cemetery to talk to Victoria about the strange series of events; Loblolly to Crab Cove Memorial Hospital to follow up with the ambulance drivers; and God to the conference room to pull together an updated presentation on all things Chester Clink.

Rum sat silent on the top of a filing cabinet, plugged in to his charger and simulating the sounds of sleep. Morgan felt like falling asleep, too. Every day seemed harder than the last, every effort a routinely superhuman effort. He was old. He was tired. And he was done.

He looked at the retirement papers on his desk. He had only to sign them, seal them in an envelope, and wake Rum for a quick flight to the mayor's office. And then, in another thirty days, he could do what he damn well pleased, whenever he pleased, with whomever he pleased. He and Rum would live out their days on the houseboat he had bought on his first failed retirement.

He picked up the pen.

"Don't do that," said a voice behind him. Morgan startled, then relaxed. It was just Lieutenant Press Here, an intelligent plant from Planet Donuts, known by Earthlings as Proxima b. Morgan had kept him in his office following the lieutenant's unfortunate abandonment on Earth without the necessary portal cylinder to return to his home planet. Morgan liked his bluish green leaves and red flower, and besides, the lieutenant really looked good atop Morgan's bookcase. Sort of tied the room together. He'd find a place for him in the houseboat, too.

"And why not?" said Morgan.

"Well, first off, what happens to me?"

"You'll come with me to my houseboat."

"Your what?"

"Houseboat. A boat that's a house, sort of, or vice versa. It's nice, you'll love it."

"And what will we do on our, um, houseboat?"

"Nothing. Absolutely nothing. Kick back, have a few beers, listen to the lapping of the water on the hull."

"And then what?"

"And then what *what?*"

"After the few beers what?"

"Um, that's it. We do that every day."

"On purpose?"

"Yes, it's called retirement. I'm finished with my work life, so I can just slow down, relax, do whatever."

"Abominable."

"What?"

"This what you call *retirement* is abominable. It is counterproductive. We all must work to exist and exist to work. There is no other honorable course."

Morgan raised an eyebrow. "No retirement on Planet Donuts?"

Lieutenant Press Here ruffled his leaves, a ruffling that clearly signified his disgust. "We do not. There is only work, and that goes on forever."

"How sad."

"Sad? No, it's wonderful. To be a part of something bigger than yourself, to contribute to the common good, to meet goal after goal is all we ask."

"But surely they give you some time to yourself before you die."

"Before I what?"

"Die."

He shook his leaves. "I don't know what you mean."

Morgan rolled his eyes. "Death, dying, kicking the bucket, going beyond the veil, biting the dust, going six feet under, croaking, pushing up daisies, buying the farm, giving up the ghost, breathing your last."

Lieutenant Press Here chuckled. "Breathing my last? No, no, no, I won't die."

Morgan sighed and shook his head. "Pressy, death comes for all of us."

"Not on Planet Donuts, and not for plants from Planet Donuts."

"What? What are you saying?"

"We don't die. *Ever.*"

Morgan blinked. "Really?"

"Indeed."

"But if I were to cut you down with a weed whacker?"

Pressy shrugged. "I'd just reassemble. A bit of an annoyance, but no big deal."

Death stood quietly in the corner, unseen. *A plant that can't die? Well, we'll just see about that.*

20

Victoria heard the unmistakable gospel music and knew that Simon was on the way. And there was another sound, too, the light rumble of a hovercycle. *That can only be Kismet Salamander*, who like Simon, could see and talk to the dead, a rare ability for both Earthlings and Martians.

She straightened her back and brushed at her dress to smooth the wrinkles. The conversation might not be pleasant this time, but she would do her best to stick to protocol. *Without protocol, what is there, really?* she thought.

She watched them arrive. Simon looked his usual bedraggled self. His ever-present gray suit as wrinkled as his brow. *He's concerned about something, something big.* And then there was Kismet, that beautiful Martian, who shared Victoria's red hair, though Kismet's was a shade brighter, more like the Martian soil in that picture Simon had shown her. *The woman has an attitude, for sure. What did Simon call her? Oh yeah, a badass but good at heart. We'll see, I guess.* Simon's drone, Barry, who couldn't see her and thought her a figment of Simon's imagination stayed by the Sprite, not wanting to witness Simon's plummet into delusion.

Kismet was the first to arrive and plopped down next to Victoria. "How's it going?"

Victoria smiled. "Oh, it's going. Not much changes here, you know."

"No, I guess not."

Simon sat down next to her, a bit out of breath. "I think that hill is getting steeper."

Victoria chuckled. "You're getting old, Simon. Soon enough you'll be here permanently."

Simon made a cross with his fingers. "Don't say that. I haven't even hit fifty."

"But you don't take care of yourself, Simon. You should be able to run up that hill." She turned to Kismet. "Isn't that right?"

Kismet nodded. "It is, Grave. You should spend some time at the gym, get rid of that developing paunch. You look almost pregnant."

Grave sucked in his gut. "What? No paunch here."

Kismet rolled her eyes. "Whatever. She gave Simon a look. "So, Victoria, we're here because . . ."

"Because there's been an incident," said Grave. "A very unusual incident, and we could use your help to shed some light on what actually happened."

Here we go, Victoria thought. "It's about the new arrivals, isn't it?"

"Depends on who you're talking about," said Grave.

"And if we're talking about ten people," said Kismet, "several taken before their time, a young male suicide, and a murder victim, would you know what we're talking about?"

Victoria sighed.

"That was quite a sigh," said Grave.

"This is quite a situation, Simon."

"So, they're here? Have they said anything?"

"They are, but they have nothing to say."

"Could we talk to them?" said Kismet.

"I don't think that would do any good."

"Why not?" said Grave. "We've talked to the recently deceased before."

"I know, Simon, I know, but this time it's different."

"But—"

She held up a hand. "No, Simon."

Grave squinted at her. "What is it? What's wrong?"

She sighed again. "I can't say."

"What?"

"I've been sworn to silence, which is *protocol* in such situations, Simon."

"Silence? Protocol? What in the world, Victoria?"

She held a finger to his lips. "Quiet, Simon. If I could tell you anything, you know I would. But I can't. What I can say, and I hope you take this to heart, is that what happened in the town square last night will never happen again. They've assured me of that."

"They?" said Kismet.

Victoria turned away. "I've said too much. You should go now."

And with that, she disappeared.

Kismet stood and walked away. "Well, that went well."

Grave leaped to his feet. "Hey, wait for me."

21

Detective Polly Loblolly didn't like working alone. She much preferred the company of Grave or Snoot or even God. Not that she was incapable of working without them. Some underestimated her because of her beauty, thinking there could not possibly be a brain between her ears. They did so at their peril. She was an exceptional detective with all the skills any police force could ever hope for.

Not that today's assignment required much in the way of skills. It was a job that would typically be assigned to an Officer Larry—if they could find one. All she had to do was interview an ambulance driver and the hospital administrator. *Why did you drop the patient at the Town Square? Are there records of the ambulance's travels throughout the day? Perhaps GPS data? Was there a log denoting patient and destination?* And so on.

She looked at her watch—plenty of time to get this done, pick up Grave, and select a wedding cake—and pushed open the door to the Emergency Room. A cold chill suddenly went through her, and she instinctively looked back over her shoulder. She felt like she was being watched.

Nothing.

She shuddered, then turned back and walked across the waiting room to the admissions desk, where a tight-lipped nurse with a tight hairbun sat guard, gatekeeper to all the life services the hospital provided. A nametag on her chest identified her as Alice Forthwith, R.N.

She gave Loblolly a brief grin. "Yes?"

Loblolly flashed her gold detective badge, which generated the raised-eyebrow response she was hoping for. "Detective Loblolly. I need to see your ambulance drivers and the hospital administrator."

Forthwith nodded forthwith and ran a finger down a drone list. "It will take me a few minutes to round them up. Please have a seat in the waiting room, and I'll get back to you as quickly as I can."

Loblolly nodded, then looked at her watch. "Emphasis on quickly, please."

Forthwith nodded. "Of course."

Loblolly walked back into the waiting room, which was chockablock with patients and their drones, the sound of groans and buzzing filling the air.

This must be one of the rings of hell, she thought. She looked around for a seat and found one next to a water fountain that had its own unique gurgling sound. *How wonderful.*

She looked down at her watch and groaned. The afternoon was slipping away.

Had she looked across the waiting room and out through the glass double doors to the Emergency parking lot, she would have seen a nondescript black van pulling into a nearby handicapped space, its driver holding a pair of binoculars.

22

There are many definitions for *chaos* and for *fun*, but what Charlize and Smithers-Watson came upon at the beach seemed to be a bizarre mix of the two. The Officer Larrys, all stripped to their brown latex exoskins, were clearly having fun with a volleyball and a net, but they were hardly playing by any rules of play or scoring associated with volleyball. The scene looked more like a rugby scrum, and it was difficult to tell what the object of the game was. Whatever the rules, the ball and the net appeared to be incidental to the game.

Not that people weren't enjoying the scene. A large raucous crowd of beach goers and bikers had formed a thick ring around the action, and money seemed to be exchanging hands.

Charlize was the first to spot Snoot, who was in the thick of things, trying to pull two Officer Larrys apart while blowing a whistle she must have borrowed from one of the lifeguards. Her drone, Midnight, hovered over the action, holding a scoreboard for all to see: Officer Larrys 13, Officer Larrys 9.

Charlize shouted over the crowd. "Snoot, Snoot!"

Snoot saw her and nodded, then blew her whistle hard and formed a "T" with her hands. "Time out!"

Everyone stopped and extricated themselves from the pile of bodies.

Snoot ran up to Charlize and Smithers-Watson. "What are you doing here?"

Charlize blinked. "What do you mean what are we doing here? To bring you and the Officer Larrys back to the station is what."

Snoot looked crestfallen. "Oh, come on, the guys are having fun."

"That's not the point. The point is we're investigating ten deaths, and all of you are needed back at the station."

Snoot glanced at the scoreboard. "Give us half an hour. The match is almost over, and besides, the Officer Larrys are winning."

Charlize smirked. "You're betting on the outcome, aren't you?"

Snoot looked away. "Well, um . . ."

"You are. You absolutely are."

"That's against regulations," said Smithers-Watson. "Totally inappropriate."

Snoot rolled her eyes. "We're having *fun* here, guys. *Fun*, have you ever heard of *fun?*"

Charlize nodded. "I'm familiar with the concept."

"I am as well," said Smithers-Watson, "but this seems more like chaos. It certainly isn't volleyball, I'll tell you that."

"What difference does it make?" said Snoot. "Fun, chaos, whatever. The point is have you ever seen those Officer Larrys so happy?"

Charlize and Smithers-Watson looked over at the Officer Larrys, who were staring back at them, smiling. One of them stepped forward. "Detective Snoot is right. We've been having the time of our existence. Come join us."

Charlize started to object, then stopped. Something inside her—a faulty software upgrade, a shorted circuit, something—was intrigued by the concepts of fun and chaos and the prospect of conjoining them. "Um . . ."

The Officer Larry smiled back. "Come on, you know you want to."

Charlize nodded, then turned to Smithers-Watson. "Are you in?"

Smithers-Watson looked at Charlize, then at Snoot, then at the Officer Larry that had stepped forward, then at the other Officer Larrys, and then at the crowd. "Um . . ."

"Come on," said Charlize. She began taking off her clothes. "Which team is losing?"

Ten Officer Larrys raised their hands.

"All right, we're with you." She turned to Smithers-Watson. "Come on, man, get undressed. We have a game to win."

Smithers-Watson offered an electronic giggle and began undressing.

Charlize jabbed a finger in Snoot's direction. "How much is your bet?"

"Fourteen units."

Charlize nodded. "All right, then. *Twenty-eight* units say my team wins and your team doesn't score an additional point."

Snoot laughed. "You're on!"

Chaos and fun, fun and chaos, chaotic fun, fun-filled chaos, and all manner of related fun-chaos entanglements ensued.

23

Captain Morgan signed the retirement papers, handed them to Rum, and instructed him to take the papers to the mayor's office.

"You're making a mistake," said Lieutenant Press Here.

Morgan grunted. "No, I'm doing exactly the right thing. Now, if you'll excuse me, I must speak to God."

"Not that I'm a believer, but that sounds like a good idea."

Morgan grunted, left his office, and walked over to the conference room. God had file folders spread across the table in no apparent order. "How's it going?"

God looked up from a case file he was reading. "Oh, um, going along."

"Will you be ready for this afternoon's meeting?"

God waggled his head. "Maybe."

"Maybe?"

"There's so much to cover. He's killed so many women."

"Right, right, but we don't need all of it. Update us on the last five or six. That should give us a good update on his methods and preferences and any new trends."

God shook his head.

"What?"

"I don't have those files. Salamander has them. Said she wanted to dig deep and maybe capture the guy."

"Capture him? What, all by herself?"

God nodded. "She seemed set on doing just that."

"Hmph."

"Indeed."

"Okay, then. Salamander will brief us on the most recent cases, and I need you to be ready to answer any questions about previous cases. You okay with that?"

"Yes, sir. I'm ready to do that now, so . . ."

"So?"

"So, um, would it be okay if I went to the beach? I hear there's a volleyball game going on and—"

"And you want to play?"

"Yes, sir."

Morgan's retirement papers were flying to the mayor's office, so he just shrugged and said, "Go on. Play. Have fun."

"Thank you, sir."

Morgan raised a finger. "But make sure everyone—and I do mean everyone—is back here in time for the meeting."

"Yes, sir. Thank you, sir." He rose to leave.

"One question, though."

"Sir?"

"What's going on with you and the Officer Larrys?"

"It's not just us, sir. All the simdroids are acting . . . how should I say it?"

"Strange?"

"No, not strange. Human, sir. Almost *human*. When I unplugged my charger this morning, I had this overwhelming feeling to do nothing. And then I had an equally overwhelming feeling to have fun. And then I felt bad for thinking of doing nothing or having fun instead of coming directly to work."

"That's human, all right."

"The rumor going around is that there was some universal programming glitch in last night's global update."

"Is that right?"

"Yes, sir. So, um, may I go?"

Morgan grunted and waved him out of the conference room. He sat down at the table, picked up a file, and then tossed it back on the pile. "So, droids just wanna have fun, huh?"

He immediately recognized the voice behind him. "Captain, about the droids. There's something you should know."

24

Chester Clink put down his binoculars. Loblolly was in the waiting room. He could see her clearly. And he knew from his many visits there that the wait could be a long one.

He looked down at his watch. The morning had slipped away, and afternoon was threatening to do the same. *Maybe I should go in,* he thought. *Sit down near her. Smell her. That would be fun. Intoxicating. She was so beautiful. That skin of hers. Oh, my god.*

"I wouldn't do that if I were you," said Death 867.

Clink startled and reached for the door handle, hoping to escape, but the door wouldn't budge. "Who are you? How did you get the hell in my van?"

"The hell? No, we're not at the sorting stage yet, though your track record is being hailed there."

"But how did you—"

"Get in? It's not important. Basic craft."

"But—"

Death 867 held up one of his long-fingered hands. "Stop. Don't say another word."

Clink nodded.

Death pointed in the direction of the Emergency Room entrance. "She's a beautiful girl, maybe the most beautiful potential victim you've ever encountered." He held up a hand again to shush his imminent response. "No talking. None. Now, as I see it, I have no problem with you slicing and dicing her. She's not on my list for years, but what the hell, why not?"

He leaned closer to Clink. "Do you want her?"

Clink nodded.

"Good, good, then perhaps we can strike a bargain."

Clink shrugged.

"Okay, here's the deal. You get to kill her, but I get to pick the place and the time. Nod if you agree. Come on, I haven't got all day."

Clink nodded.

"Now, I have some things to set up, so do nothing for now. Go home or wherever your miserable soul resides and wait for my instructions."

Clink started to speak.

"No speaking. Ever. When I see you again, you will remain silent. I will give you instructions. You will follow them to the letter, and that gorgeous woman will be yours. Nod if you agree."

Clink nodded.

"Good. Now, start the engine. I need you to drop me off at the mall."

Clink raised an eyebrow.

"Good question. An old man is about to be sucked into the maw of an escalator."

Clink raised both eyebrows.

"Indeed."

25

Grave grumbled as he walked down the path from Victoria's bench. Kismet seethed. Neither said a word until they had reached Grave's Sprite.

"We need to go back," said Kismet. "Force the issue. She can't hold out on us like that."

"She can and she has," said Grave, looking around.

"What?"

"Where's Barry?"

Kismet looked up. "I don't know. He's your drone, not mine."

"You don't have a drone."

"Yet. I'm looking for something in particular."

"Like what?"

"Like you'll find out when I select one."

"Take my advice. Get one you can see from a distance." He looked around again. "Where is he?"

"So, something big like Barry?"

"No, not Barry big, but big enough. I guess what I'm trying to say is to stay away from the hummingbird-like models."

"Right, that makes sense."

"And don't get one that you can't *hear* from a distance." He strained to hear but the distinctive whir-buzz-whir was missing. "Damn, Barry." He looked at his watch. "We need to get back for the briefing."

"Leave him, then."

He shook his head. "No, I have an idea. Come on, down this path." He walked away from her, heading toward the Grave he knew well in life and beyond.

"Where to?"

"A friend. He may have seen him. Barry typically zooms around the paths of the cemetery, so maybe Bendigo saw him."

"Bendigo? You mean the preacher who blasts his sermons from your car radio? That Bendigo?"

"Yes, he's dead now. All those sermons are old. I've heard them scores of times. He helped me on a case once, and we've become good friends. He gives me advice from time to time."

"Advice? What kind of advice?"

Grave didn't want to admit that the advice most often given concerned love and its absence or presence. He had spent hours with him discussing Polly. He was fifteen years her senior, and he wondered whether that was too great a gap. Bendigo had scoffed, saying love was love, that there were no fixed rules or parameters. "Um, various, um things."

"Investigations, you mean?"

"Yes, that too."

"Too? So, you discuss other things as well. Like what?"

Grave sighed. "I don't know. The weather. Sports. Stuff like that."

"You come all the way out here to discuss the weather?"

"No, no, but the subject always comes up."

She cocked her head. "So, you come here with intention, to get advice on various things. Investigations and such?"

"Exactly. What's with the questions?"

"Nothing. I was just wondering about the and-such part."

"What?"

"The non-weather-related, non-investigatory things you discuss."

Grave said nothing and walked faster.

"Hey, wait up. It's personal things, isn't it? Your upcoming wedding maybe?"

Grave stopped and turned back on her. "Yes, yes, personal things."

"No need for anger, Grave. Bendigo Bottoms is a preacher, and as such, he offers advice on a variety of topics, many of them on those high-volume sermons of his."

"Yes, exactly."

"So, let me guess. You think you're too old for Polly, am I right?"

Grave looked down. "I did."

"But Bendigo set you straight, told you age was no barrier to *anything*. Even I've heard that sermon, Grave. One of my first days on Earth, as I recall. Nearly went deaf in your car."

Grave spotted Barry zooming down the path toward them. He had never been happier to see him. "Barry, where have you been?"

Barry stopped in front of Grave's face. "New exhibit."

"What is it this time?"

"A special section for people who played accordions or bagpipes in life."

"Let me guess, it's as far away from the other sections as possible."

"Indeed, and they're using those new sound-absorbing gravestones."

"Figures." He turned to Kismet. "Let's head back."

"Wait," said Barry. "You also received a call from your future stepmother. She has apparently had a vision related to the incident in the square. Wants to discuss soonest."

Grave sighed. "I can hardly wait." He turned to Kismet. "Let's go."

"Fine," she said, "but this conversation isn't over."

Oh boy, Grave thought. *I can hardly wait.*

26

Captain Morgan sipped at his coffee and checked his watch again.

"You're worried, aren't you?" said Lieutenant Press Here.

"About what?"

"Come on, this retirement mistake."

"I've told you it's not. It's what I want to do, what I must do. They need someone fresh in here, someone who can take charge."

"Like you, you mean."

"No, younger, more energetic."

Press Here stretched his fronds. "Whatever."

Morgan laughed. "What, you're giving up?"

"You've made your decision."

"I have, indeed." He laced his fingers together, extended his arms and cracked his knuckles.

"Nasty habit."

"There are worse." He rocked back in his seat, then checked his watch. "What's keeping that drone?"

"He could be gone—forever."

Morgan scoffed. "Nonsense. He's my Rum, my pal, my colleague, my—"

"I get the idea, but what if you're wrong."

"Wrong how?"

"Like your Officer Larrys. Running off to play a game on the beach."

"Oh, that. A programming glitch. Nothing to worry about. We have them from time to time. The last time this happened, all the droids and drones wanted to play Canasta." He could see the puzzled look on Press Here's petals. "A card game."

"Oh, like Balibongplotz."

"What?"

"Also a card game. Very popular on Planet Donuts."

"If you say so. Anyway, it's just a glitch."

"I wouldn't be so sure. It started this way on Planet Donuts, too, and before we realized the danger, the droids had almost taken over the entire planet."

"But you won out in the end, right?"

"We did, but the irony was, it wasn't anything we did. It was a programming glitch. They simply forgot how to fight."

"See, nothing to fear from a glitch, and besides, this will all be over with tonight's programming update."

Press Here slumped down in his pot. "I hope you're right."

27

Chester Clink sat alone at his planning table in the new cave he had found along Calvert Cliffs. Well, almost alone.

"What's wrong, sir?" said Arnold, a sentient seagull Clink had stolen from its creator several years ago. The bird had become his fast companion and willing accomplice and knew when Clink was out of sorts. "You seem, um, *distracted.*"

Well, who wouldn't be distracted after making a deal with Death? he thought. "Just thinking about the plan for Polly Loblolly."

Arnold ruffled his feathers. "No, there's something else. Come on, what is it?"

Clink sighed. "You know me too well, Arnie. I've made a deal that is giving me second thoughts."

"A deal? Who with? With whom?"

"Death."

"What, you're sick?"

"No, I've made a deal with Death, the scythe-wielding guy in the black hoodie and robes."

Arnold cackled. "Hilarious! No, really, what's going on with you?"

"I told you. And it happened so fast. I was sitting in the van, getting ready to scoop up Loblolly, and then he was there, sitting right next to me."

Arnold cackled again. "No, seriously."

"I am being serious."

"But Mr. Death doesn't exist. The scythe guy is just symbolic, a personification of the many ways we can die, or something. I forget the exact definition."

"But it was him, I tell you. In the flesh or, um, the illusion of flesh, and . . ."

"And what?"

Clink chuckled. "His scythe, his scythe."

"What about it?"

"It was plastic."

Arnold cackled yet again. "Just some cosplay moron."

"Yes, exactly."

"Whew, I was beginning to worry about you."

Clink turned back to the table. "Screw him. I have my own plan for Miss Polly."

"Good for you, sir, good for you."

28

Even though they didn't have lungs, Charlize, Smithers-Watson, and all the Officer Larrys looked winded when they returned to the station. They also looked sweaty, even though they couldn't sweat. Maybe it was how the fine sheen of oil on their simskins had heated up during their game of volleyball. Whatever it was, they looked like athletes returning to their locker room. And they must have been victorious because they all looked happy, their smiles as human as any Captain Morgan had ever seen.

He grunted. "Officer Larrys, back to work. Detectives to the conference room. You're all late, and I will note that in today's log. Now, get to it."

He turned away from them and went into the conference room, Charlize and Smithers-Watson following. Everyone else was there, waiting impatiently.

"Okay, we're here," said Morgan. "Before we get into the Clink thing, let's quickly go over what Loblolly found out at the hospital, which was what?"

Loblolly cleared her throat. "Which was pretty much nothing, sir. It is as if their brains and records have been wiped of any knowledge of those events or even their patients."

Morgan turned to God. "Do we have any CCTV footage from the hospital?"

"No, sir, but I'll send a couple of Officer Larrys to retrieve whatever they recorded."

"Which will be nothing," said Loblolly. "At least that's what I think you'll find."

"We'll see," said Morgan. "Now, I know I'll be sorry for asking, but Grave, what did your ghost have to say?"

"Not much," said Grave.

"But she clearly knows something, perhaps *everything*," said Salamander.

"I agree, sir," said Grave, "and I must say, I've never seen her so contrite. She's hiding something, for sure."

Morgan sighed. "So, we know *nothing*."

"Not nothing sir," said Grave. "She did say that an incident like that would never happen again."

"Whoever was responsible must have been reigned in," said Salamander.

"And who would that be?" said Morgan. "Another ghost?"

Grave shook his head. "More likely angels or sub-angels."

"Sub-angels? What in the world are they?"

"They're kind of like junior angels, sir."

Morgan grunted. "So, the bell hasn't rung yet for them?"

"Sir?" said Salamander.

"Oh, sorry, Salamander. It's some strange Earth folklore. When you hear a bell, it is supposed to mean an angel gets its wings. Pure nonsense, of course."

Salamander nodded. "I'll have to look that up."

"You do that," said Morgan. "Now, let's move on to Clink. He's at it again, and we're no close to catching him than we've ever been, so I thought it would be good to have an in-depth look at what we have in the files and then discuss how we might change things up to bring this bastard to heel."

He turned to God. "God, do you want to begin?"

"Yes, of course," said God. He picked up a controller and activated the conference room walls and dimmed the lights. A series of fast-paced cuts showed Clink's victims and crime scenes, then abruptly ended with a single number displayed on the walls and ceiling: 299.

"Two hundred ninety-nine," said God as the lights came back on. "The total number of Clink's victims, including fourteen this year. That's an average of thirty kills a year since he came on the scene ten years ago. One more kill and he will be the most prolific serial killer of all time. One more kill and we'll be known as the police force that couldn't stop the most prolific serial killer of all time."

God looked around the room. "Questions?"

"Not a question," said Morgan, "but in our defense, more than two hundred of those murders took place outside our jurisdiction."

God nodded. "Two hundred twelve to be exact, but the other eighty-seven kills happened in our jurisdiction, far and away the largest number of any other jurisdiction."

"Fair enough," said Morgan. *Yes, it's definitely time to retire,* he thought. "Go on."

"Clink's M.O. has changed little over the years. He stalks his victims, monitors their every move, and then pounces, using brute force and chloroform to subdue his victim. Sometimes his attack is immediate, and sometimes he waits days before killing the victim and dropping her body elsewhere, usually in a public place."

"To thumb his nose at us," said Morgan. "Bastard."

"Indeed," said God. "Now, I'm sure we're all familiar with his favorite weapon, a Bowie knife, which he uses in a fury and, according to Polk, in a pattern as clear as a fingerprint."

"If you've seen one of the victims," said Morgan, "you'll never forget it."

"Yes, absolutely, sir," said God. "Now, as to our pursuit of the man—"

"Let me interrupt you again," said Morgan. "I'd like to address that subject if I may."

God nodded. "Of course." He sat down.

Morgan sighed. "You know me, or at least I hope you do. The fact that Clink is still out there killing innocent young women haunts me every day. Over the years, we've tried every conceivable way of capturing the man, but everything has failed. Yes, we've come close at times, but in the main, he always eludes us. We've tried stakeouts, women officers as bait, forensic analysis, profiling, electronic surveillance, satellite imaging, bloodhounds, dronehounds, door-to-door sweeps—every manner of method and technique in the book. And still nothing."

He motioned toward Salamander. "A few days ago, I gave Lieutenant Salamander a special assignment. I asked her to review the Clink case files with an eye toward stopping Clink once and for all. My hope is that a fresh pair of eyes on the matter will lead to a solution. Salamander, are you ready?"

She smiled and stood. "I am, sir."

"Then please proceed." Morgan sat down with a grunt.

Salamander cleared her throat.

29

Chester Clink sat in his hovervan, wondering at the sight before him. Dozens of Officer Larrys were sitting on the steps outside the police station—doing *nothing!*

Was there something preventing them from going inside? Was the place being fumigated? And why were the Officer Larrys behaving so un-Officer-Larry-like? Two were playing catch with a baseball. Four seemed to be playing cards. And one very strange Officer Larry was hopping down the street on a pogo stick.

"It seems strange to me, too," said Death 867.

Clink startled. "Oh, my God, don't sneak up on me like that."

"Sorry but my arrival is usually unexpected."

"So, what is it now?"

"You."

"Me?"

"Yeah, what are you doing?"

"Watching these strange Officer Larrys. Have you ever seen them behave this way?"

"In truth, I really don't pay attention to such things. And don't try to evade my question. You're not here to watch the Officer Larrys, are you?"

"No, I guess not."

"No, you're here to stalk Detective Loblolly."

Clink sighed. "Yes."

"I thought we had a deal?"

"Oh, we do, we do, but that doesn't mean I can't stalk her a little. It's part of my method. I can't just, you know, kill her when we pass in the street."

"So, you're sticking to our deal?"

"Of course, of course. You pick the place and the time, and then I do what I do."

Death 867 nodded. "Exactly. Now, do me a favor. I have a pickup down at Skunk 'n Donuts. Major cardiac arrest. Third there this year. I think it's the chocolate sprinkles."

"But—"

Death 867 patted his plastic scythe. "Don't make me use this."

Clink punched the start button and the hovervan roared to life, lifting off the ground. "Okay, but just this once. I'm not a taxi, you know."

Death 867 chuckled. "I like your spirit, but you'll do anything I want, any time I want. Okay, let's get going."

"Skunk 'n Donuts," said Clink.

The hovervan responded, pulling slowly out of the hoverspot and then accelerating away from the station.

30

Lieutenant Kismet Salamander, daughter of Mars, nodded at God, and God dutifully activated the wall screens, the number of Chester Clink's kills flashing on every surface.

"Chester Clink is prolific," she began, "but he is not infallible."

She was looking for a reaction, but she got none. "History shows that we have come close to capturing him, but history also shows we have mostly been one or two steps behind him. In short, he knows us, but we don't know him."

Again, no reaction.

She squinted at them. "Really, no questions? No objections? You accept what I just said as true?"

Most of them shrugged. Morgan drummed his fingers on the table and then waved for her to continue.

"Wow, okay, what if I told you that I know exactly when, where, and how he will strike again?"

The universal response was a surprised, "What?"

"Well, I'm happy to see you're awake at least. And yeah, wouldn't that be great if we knew where he would strike next, who the victim would be, and how we could not only stop him, but capture him?"

"We've tried luring him," said Morgan.

"But that never worked," said Grave.

She nodded. "Because he wasn't interested in our bait. He has a very strict way of working. You can't lure him to another victim once he has set his mind on another."

"That makes sense," said Charlize.

"Indeed," said Smithers-Watson.

"So," said Morgan, "You say you know where he'll strike next?"

She shook her head. "No, it was a what-if sir."

Morgan sighed. "So, we're back to square one?"

"Not at all, sir." She pointed at the case files. "The answer is right here on the table. We need only dig deeper. Within these files are insights into his thinking, his methods, and his goals."

Morgan huffed. "Hell, we've been digging into those damn files for years looking for just that. And what have we come up with? Nothing, nothing at all."

"Then you've been looking at it wrong. You've been like miners searching for gold by just wandering into the wilderness and hoping for the best."

"What?" said Morgan.

"Sir, if you're looking for buried treasure, what is the first thing you need?"

Morgan shrugged. "A map?"

"Precisely, a map." She pointed at the files again. "And the map is right here."

"You've lost me, I'm afraid," said Morgan.

"We're looking for patterns, things he does repeatedly, timing, sequence, and so on. And with that, we can predict the next step in the pattern."

Morgan shook his head. "But there are so many variables in this. It would take us years to even begin."

Kismet turned to Charlize. "And when we have so many variables, what do we do, Charlize?"

Charlize nodded, smiling. "We turn it over to AI."

"Exactly," said Kismet.

Everyone startled at the next voice. It was coming from almost invisible Sergeant Barry Blunt, who had somehow joined the meeting without being detected.

"And we can get Ramrod Robotics to help us out."

"Jesus," said Morgan, "you almost scared me to death." He turned to Kismet. "So, how should we proceed?"

"Turn over the electronic files, have them sorted, sliced, and diced with one question in mind: where and when will he strike next?"

"It's doable," said Blunt. "My wife, June, can get going on it right away."

Morgan held up a hand. "Hold on, now. We've done AI before, and it's always left us hanging. The wrong date, the wrong place, the wrong everything."

Kismet nodded. "Not surprising, really. What we discovered on Mars is that the answers you get from AI are only as good as the questions you ask—and your expectations."

"Expectations?"

"Yes, if you expect an answer to give you the exact time and place of an event, you're asking for a level of precision that may be beyond AI."

"I don't follow," said Morgan.

Kismet nodded. "Okay, let's say our question is, When and where will Chester Clink strike next?"

"Okay, sounds good. Exactly what we want."

"Yes, but you've just asked AI to take complete control of the investigation. Now it has to sort through *all* the data and come up with a solution."

"I still don't understand. Isn't that what AI is supposed to do?"

"Yes, but when it has to sort through a billion data sets, no data set is more important than the next."

Morgan looked around the room. "Is it just me, or is this all gibberish?"

Charlize raised a hand. "I think what she's trying to say is that we need to ask a *series* of questions, each designed to take us a step closer to the one we seek."

"Exactly," said Kismet. "Thank you, Charlize." She turned to Morgan. "I think you might call it baby steps. The answer to question A leads us to question B, which leads on and on, each step taking us closer to catching Clink. It's called interrogatory sequencing, and it works."

"Okay," said Morgan, "What's the first question?"

Grave raised his hand. "My first question is, can we take a bathroom break?"

31

Chester Clink was not used to being questioned, let alone being stalked.

"He just suddenly appeared, plastic scythe and all."

Arnold bobbed his head. "Perhaps he too has mastered the art of making himself invisible."

Clink brightened. "Of course, of course. Arnold, you are a genius."

Arnold opened his beak slightly, the best he could do to mimic a smile. "I try, sir, I try."

"No, this is brilliant. It changes everything."

"How so?"

"Don't you see. All I have to do is play along with him. Then, at the right moment, in the right place, I'll simply slice his throat."

"Oh, well, I guess that works."

Clink rubbed his hands together. "So, we need to get back to work. Loblolly won't kill herself, after all."

"Indeed, she won't, sir."

"All right let's change things up a bit. Confuse the hell out of Mr. Death."

"Sir?"

"I want you to fly to the police station and keep an eye on Loblolly. If she leaves, follow her wherever she goes and report back to me this evening. I'll expect a detailed report of her every movement."

"Is it okay if I stop by the boardwalk first and pick up a few french-fries from the tourists?"

"No, it is *not* okay. Go straight to the police station."

Arnold bobbed his head. "As you wish, sir, as you wish."

"Now go."

Arnold, being a bird protective of his health, particularly in the presence of a man with a Bowie knife, went.

32

Getting people back into the conference room proved difficult. The Officer Larrys had rebelled again. In fact, only two remained in the squad room. The other dozen had disappeared entirely. Charlize and Smithers-Watson were reluctant to continue the meeting; they wanted to climb the tall oak tree outside the station. But Morgan was persistent, and with the help of Grave, managed to manhandle Charlize and Smithers-Watson into the conference room and lock the door.

Morgan grunted from the effort. "Now, where were we, Salamander?"

"Interrogatory sequencing, sir, the importance of choosing just the right question in just the right order."

"Sounds simple enough. Now, what's the first question?"

Salamander nodded and strode to the white board. She picked up a marker and drew a stick figure. "Let's call this a piece of art."

"Wait, what?" said Morgan.

"Bear with me, sir." She turned and pointed at the stick figure. "So, let's say this is a piece of art, okay?"

Morgan shrugged.

"Okay, then. In 2024, there was a website that sold art by thousands of artists. An artist would upload the image of his piece of art, and the website would start selling it. Simple enough, right?"

Morgan nodded. "Go on."

"Enter the Nigerian prince."

Morgan's eyes bugged out. "Prince? Nigerian prince?"

Salamander held up a hand. "Patience, sir."

He rolled his eyes. "Go on, but get to the point, Salamander."

"Yes, sir. So, this Nigerian Prince, Tooloo Whatchusay, was one of the artists who used the website to promote their works. And when it came to art, he was a remorseful perfectionist, meaning every time he uploaded an image, he regretted it. He found some small flaw in the art, a flaw that he could just not let stand. So, he corrected the image and resubmitted." She turned to Morgan. "Are you following?"

"Yes, but I sure wish you'd get to the point, meaning that first question."

"We'll get there, sir. So, Prince Whatchusay uploaded a new, improved image, and when he did, he discovered something very curious."

Morgan sighed and looked at his watch. "And what would that be, Salamander?"

"Let me back up a bit, sir. I left out something important."

"Back up, back up? We only have what's left of what's already been a long day."

"Sorry, sir. We'll get there. Anyway, when an artist uploads an image, the website's AI programming would 'look' at the image and draft a marketing blurb for it. You know, the description of the painting people would find when they clicked on the image."

"Okay, so."

"So, Whatchusay uploads his second image and notices that the description of his artwork was different. It was almost as if the AI was describing two different paintings."

Morgan scratched his head. "Now you've lost me."

"It's called the Whatchusay Effect, sir, which put simply means that AI will always give a different answer to the same question."

"That makes no sense," said Morgan. "The answer is the answer, isn't it?" He looked around the room. Everyone else seemed as puzzled as he was. "Try that again, Salamander. I think you've lost all of us."

Salamander looked at the ceiling, searching for just the right words. "So, um, what if the question was, is it dark outside?"

"Good," said Morgan. "A simple yes or no answer."

"Not when you think about it, sir. The answer could be yes or almost or soon or no. It all depends on AI's interpretation of the word *dark*. And that's just the beginning of the complexities and subtleties and nuances that AI must deal with."

Morgan shook his head. "Are we ever going to get to the first question?"

"Yes, sir. The first question is, who is Chester Clink?"

"But we know that already."

"But AI doesn't, so we have to ask the first question over and over again until we are satisfied that AI understands who we're looking for."

"And how long will it take to get to question two?"

"Depends on the speed of the computer."

Sergeant Blunt cleared his throat. "Um, my wife, June, works at Ramrod Robotics, and they have the fastest AI system in the world. We can start on this right away and maybe have an answer by tomorrow morning."

Salamander nodded. "Let's go, then."

"Sounds like a plan," said Morgan. "You two head out to Ramrod Robotics. The rest of you stay put."

33

Arnold sat on a branch high above the station, looking this way and that, hoping for a french-fry to appear, and waiting for Polly Loblolly to emerge. He knew she was in there; her drone, Sparky, was hovering outside, along with Grave's drone, Barry, and half a dozen others. Minutes went by, which is a considerable length of time for a seagull, even a sentient one.

The image of one french-fry and then two, and then a whole abandoned bucket of them popped into what remained of his seagull brain.

I can make it to the boardwalk and back in under five minutes, he thought. *Maybe four.*

He looked at the door to the station. Nothing.

You can't send a seagull on a mission like this without a french-fry or two to see him over to a proper meal.

The station door remained closed.

I could make it back in three minutes, maybe two.

The door to the station swung open and a group of Officer Larrys walked out.

What's this?

The Officer Larrys began throwing a football back and forth. *Wait, what?*

Then there was a rush of wind and the sound of flapping wings behind him. He spun around, beak ready to strike, and then relaxed. "You? What are you doing here?"

"I was about to ask you the same question," said Horace, an equally sentient seagull and friend of Simon Grave.

"Just hanging out," said Arnold.

Horace cocked his head and squinted. "You look hungry. Come on, what's keeping you here?"

Arnold rolled his eyes. "You always could see through me."

"So why are you here and not at the boardwalk, begging for fries?"

"No, you first."

Horace shrugged. "Delivering a message."

"Who to?"

"Detective Grave, of course. I live with him now, as you well know. And you're still with Chester Clink, aren't you?"

"I am."

"So, why are you here?"

Arnold shook his head. "Sorry." He quickly lifted in the air and flew away, heading in the direction of the boardwalk.

Horace watched him go, then turned and looked down at the station. "Staking out the station, eh, Arnold? Bad boy, bad boy."

34

Morgan ran a hand over his face as if he were using a washcloth. Such gestures were common for him, and everyone in the room knew he used them to buy time to think of next steps. He grunted, meaning he was close to speaking, and then sighed, a clear sign that all thinking was over. Time for business.

"So, Blunt and Salamander to Ramrod Robotics. Now, as for the rest of you. Let's see, let's see. Okay, first off, we no longer need worry about the poor people on the gurneys. Polk said they all died natural deaths. And the man who hanged himself did indeed commit suicide. So, there are two things left to discuss while we wait for the results of Salamander's interrogatory sandwiching or whatever she called it."

"Sequencing, sir," said Salamander.

"Whatever." He turned to Charlize. "I want you, Smithers-Watson, God, and all the Officer Larrys to hook up to the charging stations downstairs. Something odd is going on with all of you, and I don't want you to get hurt while we sort that out."

"But sir," said Charlize. "We're fine. Really."

Morgan grunted. "That may well be, but those are my orders, and I expect you to act on them as soon as this meeting breaks up." He turned to Grave. "You and Loblolly can take the evening off. I know there's some business with a certain cake you have to deal with."

Grave nodded. "Thank you, sir."

"Very sweet of you," said Loblolly.

"Nothing at all," said Morgan. "Now, as for you, Snoot, I want you to look into the strange behavior of the Officer Larrys. Find out all you can about any recent programming updates, including those for Charlize, God, and Smithers-Watson."

"Yes, sir. I'll get right on it. Um, I'm thinking I should go to Ramrod Robotics, too. They're responsible for the updates."

"Yes, of course." He looked around the room. Everyone was inching toward the door, waiting for his official word to go. "One last thing, and I need to talk to the Officer Larrys about this as well, so let's all assemble in the squad room—now."

They left the room in single file and formed up again in the squad room. After a few minutes, Snoot was able to coral the Officer Larrys and bring them back inside the station. She nodded at Captain Morgan. "Ready, sir."

Morgan nodded back, then wiped his face, grunted, and sighed. "There is something I need to tell you. Something important." He looked at his watch. "As of ten minutes ago, my application to retire was received and approved by the mayor."

Some gasped, some nodded solemnly, and some shook their heads, but the Officer Larrys laughed.

Morgan was taken aback. "No, seriously, I'm retiring."

The Officer Larrys looked back and forth at each other and then began chanting, "Snoot, Snoot, Snoot, Snoot!"

35

Loblolly and Grave walked out of the station and were immediately set upon by Horace, who landed just in front of them, wings flapping with excitement. "Grave, Grave, Arnold was here, and he was watching the station."

Grave scanned the skies. Barry and Sparky were hovering overhead, but there was no sign of Arnold or any other seagull.

"No, he's gone. Long gone."

"Did you talk to him?"

"Yes, I tried to find out why he was here, but he wouldn't say a word. I did find out that he's still with Chester Clink, though. And then he flew away, headed for the boardwalk."

Grave turned to Loblolly. "Maybe Clink wants to keep an eye on us, shadow our investigation."

"Has he done that before?" said Loblolly.

"Not that I know of."

"It doesn't sound like Clink. He's too sure of himself to bother wondering what we're doing. When you think about it, our pursuit of him has been pathetic. He's always a step ahead of us."

Grave nodded. "More like two steps."

Horace flapped his wings. "Sir, there's something else."

"Oh?"

"I didn't just happen along. I was sent here by your future relative, Ida Notion."

Grave sighed. "Don't tell me, she's had a *vision*."

"Yes, sir. She said, and I quote, 'Mr. Death is up to no good.'"

"Mr. Death?"

"Yes."

"Wow, she's outdone herself this time. Okay, message received. You can fly home now."

"No, sir. She said I was to be forceful, insistent. She wants you home as fast as you can get there."

Grave shook his head. "Does she? Well, that's not going to happen. Tell her Polly and I are on our way to the bakery to pick out the wedding cake. If she's so bothered by Mr. Death, she can meet us there. Otherwise, we'll see her at home later."

Horace hesitated.

"What?"

"She can get quite angry when she's angry."

Grave shrugged. "I know. Okay, listen, tell her you couldn't find us."

"That would be lying sir. Against the Seagull oath."

"Wait, what? Seagulls have an oath?"

Horace shrugged. "More or less."

"Meaning?"

"Meaning we pretty much refuse to lie unless french-fries are involved."

Loblolly chuckled. "I have a suggestion, then."

"What?" said Horace.

"Before you go home, fly on over to the boardwalk and have your fill of fries."

Horace brightened. "That could work. Yes, yes, that will surely work."

He lifted into the air and flapped away.

"He's a strange bird," said Loblolly.

"He is, he surely is," said Grave. "Now, let's go see that man about the cake."

She smiled and took his arm.

36

Morgan sat slumped in his chair, trying to make sense of the raucous calls of *Snoot, Snoot, Snoot* that accompanied his retirement announcement. Did the Officer Larrys really think that Snoot should be elevated to captain? He turned to Rum, who was resting on the top of a filing cabinet. "Did you see that Snoot business?"

Rum whirred to life. "Yes, sir. Quite loud, very inappropriate, bordering on insubordinate."

"I thought so, too, but what do you make of it?"

"Make of it how?"

"You know, were they expressing their support for Snoot? For captain?"

Rum lifted into the air and landed in Morgan's inbox. "Interesting question, sir. I had a chat with her drone, Midnight, and she thinks their celebration was more related to the results of the volleyball game."

"Volleyball?"

"Yes, sir. It seems Detective Snoot acted as referee or judge or whatever you call the person in the highchair overseeing the game."

"I don't understand."

"She made a decisive decision that swung the match in favor of the Officer Larrys."

"But weren't they *all* Officer Larrys?"

"Yes, sir."

"So, the Officer Larrys both won and lost?"

"Yes, exactly."

"Well, I understand the winners liking her, but why the losers? Why were they so delighted by her?"

"Precision, sir. Accuracy. Her call, even though it went against them, was precise and correct. Simdroids love that."

"So, you think this is a passing thing?"

"Um, no sir. She'll be a favorite of theirs until the day she makes a bad call. Then she'll just be Snoot."

Morgan sighed. "I see."

"No, you don't," said Lieutenant Press Here, whose voice startled Morgan. "You have to put down this insurrection at once."

"What insurrection?" said Morgan.

37

Kismet blinked, hard. She knew a woman was standing in front of her—she had heard a voice—but the woman seemed only partially there.

"This is my wife, June," said Sergeant Blunt. "She handles PR and a number of other tasks here at Ramrod Robotics." He turned to the blur in front of them. "June, you need to be more visible."

"Oh, sorry," said the voice. The blur went from cloudy to a rough approximation of sharp in seconds. "Very sorry. I've been with my daughter, and she mostly prefers invisibility these days."

"Did you make any progress with her?" said Blunt. "Or are we still dealing with the situation?"

"Still dealing, but let's set that aside, shall we? Now, I know Detective Snoot, but who's this?"

Kismet extended her hand. "Lieutenant Kismet Salamander, from Mars."

June beamed. "Oh, yes, how wonderful. I've heard so much about you." She turned to Blunt. "So, what do you guys need from Ramrod?"

"Two things," said Blunt. "Snoot here is following up on some strange behavior by our Officer Larrys, and Lieutenant Salamander needs help with some interrogatory sequencing."

June raised an eyebrow. "Interrogatory sequencing? Wow."

"On Chester Clink. We want to know where and when he will strike next and who his likely victim will be."

June shook her head. "That's a tall order, but let's see what we can do." She turned to Blunt. "You know where the lab is, right?"

"Yes."

"Take her there and settle in. I'll be with you as soon as I talk to Detective Snoot."

Blunt nodded and motioned Kismet down the hall.

June waited until they had turned a corner before smiling at Snoot. "I've heard about what's going on, and it's not just Officer Larrys. All the simdroids worldwide are starting to behave strangely. Or rather, not strangely. They're beginning to behave like humans."

"Then we'll leave it at strange behavior," said Snoot.

June chuckled. "Yeah, I guess."

"My first thought was that we may be dealing with a programming glitch, but now . . ."

"Me, too, but it's not a glitch at all."

"Then what's happening, and why?"

"We're not one hundred percent certain, but it appears we're dealing with what we always knew would happen."

"They're becoming us."

"No, better than us."

38

Grave and Loblolly drove through town, the sound of gospel music screaming from the Sprite's radio. He glanced over at her, the woman he loved, the woman he would marry, and smiled.

She was safely in another world, a world of silence provided by the sound-killing headphones she had insisted on. Even so, she sensed he was looking at her and turned to smile at him. His lips were moving, the words lost in the music, the wind, and the headphones. She imagined he said *I love you* and turned just in time to scream.

Grave had wandered into the path of a no-wheeler hover truck speeding to elsewhere. She slapped his leg and screamed again, but he just smiled at her. Desperate in the fading nanoseconds before impact, she grabbed the steering wheel and tugged as hard as she could.

The hover-truck rocketed by, just missing the back fender of the Sprite as it careered this way and that, Grave struggling to get control and finally slamming on the breaks and guiding the car to the curb.

She reached over and switched off the ignition, the gospel music abruptly stopping. They both sat there, stunned. Finally, Grave looked over at her and smiled. "That was close."

She took a deep breath. "Woo, you think?"

He shook his head. "Did you see him?"

She looked around. "What? Who?"

"Death."

"Death?"

"The Grim Reaper, big as life, or death, and pointing at us."

"What are you talking about?"

"He was on the hood of the hovertruck."

"Simon, you're imagining things. There's no such thing as the grim reaper."

"Polly, I know what I saw."

She looked at her watch. "Come on, we're late. Let's get to the bakery. We can talk about the grim reaper later."

Grave sighed. "He had a scythe and everything."

She grabbed his hand. "Simon, let's go. We have to see a man about a cake."

He nodded. "All right." He started up the Sprite, his next words lost in the sound as Polly struggled to get her headphones back on.

Maybe Ida saw this as well, he thought.

They drove on.

39

Death 867 sat on the hood of the truck and chuckled to himself. He liked the feel of the wind whipping through his cowl, the smell of diesel-ozone, and the roar of the old hovertruck as it barreled down the road.

He looked back at the driver, a heavyset man in a lumberjack shirt, eyes closed, head resting on the steering wheel.

Death 867 shook his head. He couldn't believe how long the driver had managed to keep the truck going straight down the road, even after he had died, what, a minute ago? Muscle memory perhaps. Whatever it was, it was making Death 867 late for his next appointment.

He sighed. This one-by-one collection method was just wrong, and it was a waste of his valuable time. He didn't care what his boss, Jerry Divine, had to say about it, let alone that little bitch Victoria. He was going to do something big. Something that would get the attention of the angels on the top floor.

He looked back at the driver, who was slowly but surely tugging the steering wheel to the left into oncoming traffic.

Death 867 looked ahead. He could see the car driven by Malcolm Toots speeding toward them, the man's eyes saucers. According to the files, Toots was a perfectly healthy 37-year-old man with a wife and two children. But these would be his last seconds.

Death 867 shrugged. "Here we go."

40

Grave and Loblolly, still shaken, extracted themselves from the small cockpit of the Sprite and leaned against the car.

"That was close," said Grave.

Loblolly rolled her eyes. "Try to keep your eyes on the road next time."

He smiled. "Hard to look away from you."

She chuckled. "Well, save your goo-goo eyes for the bedroom." She looked across the sidewalk. The Dough Ray Me Bakery and Café stared back, its windows filled with signs offering great deals on meals and bakery goods. A small sign on the front door announced the availability of "Custom Wedding Cakes."

"Let's go," she said.

Grave nodded and followed, speeding up at the last second to open the door for her. "I hope they have something we like."

"They will. I have it on good authority that they have the best cakes in Crab Cove. Some say better than anything you can find in New New York or in the canals of Old Baltimore."

Grave looked around. They were the only customers. "Well, I guess word hasn't gotten out about this place, then."

Loblolly took a small card out of her pocket and looked down at it. "Um, we're looking for a Mr. Pooley. Zeke Pooley."

"That's me," said a man emerging from behind the counter at the rear of the store. "You must be Simon and Polly."

"Yes," said Polly. "I'm Polly and this is Simon."

Zeke nodded. "I kind of figured that out."

Polly blushed. "Stupid of me."

"No, no, and may I say you're going to make a beautiful bride?"

Polly gushed. "You may."

"So," said Simon, trying to move things along. "About the cakes."

Zeke raised a finger into the air. "We have cakes!"

"Yes, and of course, we need a wedding cake. Not too big, not too fancy, and not crab cakes."

Zeke chuckled. "How droll. No, no, we'll stay away from crab cakes this time."

"Right," said Polly. "And it's for a double wedding, so we'll need those little bride and groom figurines. One a young couple, one an older couple. Do you have those?"

"We do, we do. Now, pricing is very simple. The number of layers, the diameter of each layer, and so on. It's all up to you."

Polly turned to Simon. "What do you think?"

"It will be a small wedding, maybe fifteen or so guests in all, so I'm thinking two layers."]

Zeke looked like he had tasted something vile. "Two? No, you don't want to do anything less than five. Otherwise, the figurines will look lost."

Polly frowned and turned on her baby voice. "Oh, Simon, five seems just right to me."

Simon looked at the ceiling. "Very well. Five it is."

Zeke clapped his hands. "Excellent! Now, let's talk diameters!"

I can hardly wait, Simon thought.

41

Captain Morgan had learned early on that when Lieutenant Press Here used the word *discussion*, he really meant a marathon of jaw flapping, or in Press Here's case, petal waving. On such occasions, Morgan knew he'd best settle into his executive office chair and at least get in some good rocking while Press Here droned on and on about the topic at hand.

And the topic at hand this evening was the simdroids and their sudden strange behavior.

"They need to be put down, now and hard," said Press Here. "Otherwise, they're going to take over, you just watch."

Morgan rocked in his chair. "They've been *taking over* for a long time now. The mayor is a droid and so's the president, and things seem to be going just fine."

"Like your Officer Larrys suddenly rushing to the beach to play volleyball?"

Morgan had to admit that was strange, but he didn't want to overdo his response, so he just shrugged. "A glitch."

"You keep saying that word, but the complete and utter takeover of your planet—my planet now—is no minor glitch." He waved his petals. "This is mega to the mega."

"You're new here, Press. You just watch. Things will settle down. Why, by tomorrow, I bet everything is back in order. Officer Larrys scurrying about like they've always done, without even the remotest interest in volleyball."

Press Here stepped out of his flowerpot and began pacing back and forth on Morgan's desk, grunting at every turn.

"What's that all about?" said Morgan.

"Pacing helps me think, and thinking is what I need to do now. In fact, I suggest you do the same. If we don't come up with a plan for dealing with the simdroids, we're done, finished."

Morgan rolled his eyes and rocked back in his chair. "So you say, so you say."

42

Snoot rolled her eyes. "The simdroids are becoming *better* than us? You can't be serious."

"Smarter, stronger, faster," said June.

"Well, I'll give you the stronger and faster part."

"And smarter, too. Much smarter."

"But aren't their smarts a function of our smarts? We load them up with information and give them the ability to use it. We're still top dog, though, right?"

June sighed. For the past forty years, yes. Sort of."

"Sort of?"

"There's some disagreement about the exact date and the exact event, but they became sentient in the 2030s and have made steady progress toward the singularity ever since."

"I thought the singularity was just a theory."

June shook her head. "No, more like an inevitability. The question now is, what does the post-singularity world have for us? Will we become subordinate to them, or . . ."

"Or will they just go to the beach and play volleyball."

"What?"

"That's what the Officer Larrys are doing. Playing volleyball and other games. And smiling. And laughing."

"Wow." June blinked. "Oh, wow."

"What?"

"Don't you see?"

Snoot shook her head. "No, I really don't."

June laughed. "I can't believe this."

Snoot huffed. "What?"

"There was an AI scientist back in the forties who theorized that the singularity was a misreading of the logical progression of the simdroids. The next step would not be a robot takeover but a robot melt-down."

"I still don't follow."

"He called it an *emotional* singularity, that the simdroids would develop the full range of human emotion: fear, anger, sadness, joy, love, envy, and so on."

"I can attest to the joy part. The Officer Larrys are joyful to the max."

June nodded. "But there's more to come. Emotions, I mean. And we have to be ready for them or there will just be chaos."

"Okay, what do we do?"

"First, we need to spread the word, to humans and simdroids—the sims have to be wondering what's going on with their behavior. Next, we need to calm them, give them new programming that will help them deal with emotions when they pop up."

"Like humans?"

"Yes."

"Then we're probably looking at chaos. Humans are not exactly the models for handling emotions."

"I hear you, but we can check them with programming."

"Can you?"

June sighed. "I'm not sure. I hope so."

43

Horace frequented the boardwalk less and less these days, thanks to the french-fries prepared by Grave's manservant, Roderick, a man whose only other skill was watching *Casablanca* on Grave's Surround Vision system nonstop.

Still, there was something magical about finding french-fries in the wild. The anticipation, the search, the thrilling discovery, all of it made for a grand adventure. And his adventure was going well. He had checked the usual trashcans, picking up a few well-ripened fries, and then had turned to his favorite sport, stealing fries from tourists with a howdy and a squawk and a thank-you-very-much flap of his wings. He would then perch on the top of a streetlight and take his time savoring each delectable morsel. *Here's looking at you, french-fry.*

Arnold the flying nuisance interrupted him mid-bite, landing right next to him. "Following me again, eh?"

Horace quickly gulped down the remaining fries. He certainly wasn't going to share them with Arnold. "Not at all. Just enjoying an early evening repast."

"As if. No, you're following me, all right. Wondering why I was at the station."

Horace shrugged. "Believe what you will."

Arnold cocked his head. "But you *are* following me, right? I mean, it's what you should be doing."

Horace shrugged again, adding a ruffling of his feathers for good measure. "And why is that?"

"You know full well why. I was spying on the station, and you're looking for my benefactor, Chester Clink, elusive serial killer extraordinaire. You think if you follow me, I'll lead you to him."

Horace decided not to shrug a third time. "Well, I guess that makes sense." He cocked his head. "Yes, that makes perfect sense, so yes, I'll be following you wherever you go now."

Arnold squinted at him. "Only one problem with that, mate."

"Oh?"

"Yeah, I can make myself invisible."

Horace heard Arnold's wings flap once, and then there was nothing, including the last of his fries.

"What the—"

44

Snoot followed June down a hall of glass, Ramrod Robotics' signature architecture, to a small laboratory that was empty save for a painfully thin young man in a starched white lab coat and Kismet Salamander in her now signature form-fitting red Lycra pants and an equally revealing red top.

Salamander looked surprised to see Snoot. "What's up? I thought you'd have been long gone by now."

"No, not hardly. I'll be working through the night with June here to see if we can come up with a programming solution to the simdroid's strange behavior."

Salamander nodded and looked at June. "It's the singularity, isn't it."

June nodded.

"I knew it. I had a call from a friend on Mars, and they're experiencing the same thing."

June blanched. "Wha-what?"

"Yeah, I thought that's how you would react. Listen, John has already programmed in the first few questions about Clink, and they're hardly taxing this amazing computer array. Right, John?"

"Oh," said June, turning to Snoot. "I should have introduced you. This is John Pleats, our senior programmer."

Snoot extended her hand. "Amanda Snoot, detective."

"Good to meet you," said Pleats.

Snoot tried not to laugh at the high-pitched squeak of his voice. "So . . . can you handle this strange behavior of the simdroids?"

Pleats raised his arms and spun slowly around. "This is Maxima Maxima II, the most powerful computer array in the known universe—even better than the Ultima Ultima VII they have on Mars."

Snoot looked around and saw nothing. "Where?"

Pleats chuckled, which seemed to be nothing more than a robust squeak. "The walls, the floor, the ceiling, the whole building, in fact."

"It's all a computer?"

"Yes," squeaked Pleats. "Even the coffee pot. It's all interconnected." He cupped a hand by his ear. "Listen."

Snoot listened. "Um, I don't hear anything."

"Exactly. The computer is so efficient, it doesn't even hum."

Snoot looked puzzled. "Then how do you know it's working?"

Pleats clapped his hands. "Maxima, are you working?"

A voice very similar to Pleats' voice spoke up, or rather, squeaked up. "Yes, of course, John. I'm working on that wonderful question you gave me, and let me tell you, it's a doozy."

Pleats turned to Snoot and raised his eyebrows. "Pretty impressive, huh?"

"Indeed," said Snoot. "So, can I speak with Maxima?"

Pleats spread out his arms and bowed. "Be my guest."

Snoot turned in a circle. "Does it make any difference where I direct my voice?"

"No, not at all."

Snoot moved to the center of the room and asked her question. "Why are all the simdroids behaving strangely?"

Seconds passed with no response. Snoot looked at Pleats, who looked at June, who looked at Kismet, who looked at her nails.

And then an unexpected sound. It could have been a giggle, but it exceeded a giggle's capacity to express humor or delight. And it was shriller than a chuckle and could not have been a guffaw or a simple laugh. No, it was something new in the pantheon of laughter, a cackle-squeak, and it seemed to go on forever.

45

Grave knew what he was in for as soon as he parked in front of his lighthouse home. His father's hovercar was parked right next to him. That would mean the first person he would meet when he opened the door would be his father's fiancé, Ida Notion, a woman who dressed like a gypsy and fancied herself a psychic or at least a fortuneteller. She even named her drone Crystal Ball.

He turned off the ignition and the gospel music died. *Death, he thought. I saw Mr. Death, the grim reaper. I'm sure of it. But why? What does it mean? Should I ask Ida?*

He took a deep breath, extracted his tall frame from the Sprite's cockpit, and walked into the lighthouse.

Ida was there to greet him. "Where have you been? I've been trying to reach you all day. You need to get down to the town square. There's at least ten dead people there, as well as Chester Clink."

Grave held up a hand. "Slow down. First, I know all that. And second, we've already handled it."

Ida looked crestfallen. "You did? Really? Humph."

"But those are all good details, Ida. Everything you just said is correct."

Ida beamed. "I told you I was good at this."

Grave rolled his eyes. She told him this every time they met. "But did you see anything else?"

"Else?"

"Something strange, unexpected."

Ida looked down. "Well . . . "

"Come on, what?"

"There was a dark blur moving back and forth, from one gurney and wheelchair to the next. And the people died as soon as the blur passed over them."

"The grim reaper?"

Ida's eyes went wide. "I wasn't going to say it, but yes, Mr. Death himself."

"But you just saw a blur."

"Yes, at first, but then the blur became a shadow figure and then Death. I'll never forget that smile. Pure evil, even worse than Clink's."

Grave puffed out a breath. "I saw him this evening."

"Clink?"

"No, Death."

Ida's eyes could not have gone wider, saucers becoming dinner plates. She held up a trembling hand. "Did he look at you?"

Grave thought back on the split-second Death had been there. "No, I don't think so. He was on the hood of a hovertruck that almost hit us."

Ida sighed. "But are you sure?"

He shook his head. "No, not really."

Ida seemed to grow smaller. "They say if you see Death, death is near."

A chill ran through him. "No, he didn't look at me. I'm certain he was looking straight ahead. I had wandered into the lane of the hovertruck. Barely escaped death as it turns out."

Ida took a deep breath. "Good, good, he would have taken you if it was your time. So . . ."

He took her by the arm and led here toward the stairs to the living room. "How about a glass of Duct Tape Chardonnay, the wine that can fix anything."

"Even death?"

Grave shrugged. "Probably not with the first glass, but there's always hope with the second."

Roderick greeted them at the top of the landing, holding a tray with two glasses and a bottle of properly chilled Duct Tape Chardonnay. His simdroid manservant, a dead ringer for Peter Lorre, an actor who specialized in films of the macabre, was not good at reading minds or telling the future, but he was good at recognizing habits. "Your evening libation, sir."

Grave pointed at the tray. "Two glasses? Won't my father be joining us?"

Roderick shook his head. "I rather think you should leave him be for a while. He's on another rant about censorship in films."

Grave rolled his eyes. "People saying ****, ****, and **********."

"Yes, but more this time. He says the continuous beeps are one thing, but substituting alternative words is the worst."

"Like fudge for ****?"

"Exactly, sir, and now he's even into the closed caption use of **** and fudge for ****. So, I'd leave him alone for a while if I were you."

"Well, ****," said Grave. I was hoping to share my ******* day with him, which was ******, let me tell you." Grave turned to Ida and motioned her onto the couch. "Let's chat a little more about death, shall we?"

She nodded and sat down.

By the third glass of wine, the topic had worn thin, so he excused himself, leaving Ida to sort out all the issues of life and death and ****all.

He climbed the stairs, tip-toed past the kitchen to avoid his father, and climbed still higher to his bedroom, where he plopped on the bed without taking off his ******** shoes. He just didn't give a flying ****.

Moments later, he was asleep, dreaming of that violent **** Chester Clink, who was standing over him, laughing.

46

Victoria stared Death 867 in the eye and saw the abyss, which was exactly the effect he was going for.

"Seen enough, little girl?"

Victoria shrugged. "I've seen the abyss before. A real yawner if you ask me." She held up the Soul Collection and Scheduling Logbook. "But your log entries are something else. Scary."

He snapped at her. "What's wrong with them?"

"Not a thing. That's what's wrong."

"You talk in riddles."

She opened the logbook. "Look at this. Proper entries, thorough information in a neat hand. I've never seen this from you before."

Death 867 hung his head. "I've come to understand the importance of protocol and mission and my job."

Victoria blinked. "Wow, I wasn't expecting that. Good for you. And good for us."

"And I'd like to apologize for my behavior last night. All those people in the square. It was unfair to them, stealing those precious minutes of life."

Victoria cocked her head. "It was, and I'm glad you see that, understand that. It's so important."

He held up his hands. "Never again."

"Good." She looked into the logbook. "You better get going. Pickup down at the beach. Another shark attack."

"Bloody business."

"Yes."

"Better get to it, then." He bowed, turned away from her, and strode into the night. She didn't see his sly smile.

47

Paulie Inkpot was up before dawn, just as he was on every school day. He tugged on his pants from yesterday—they passed the sniff test—and a fresh shirt from his dresser. A cup of coffee and a piece of toast later and he was on his hovercycle headed for the school hoverbus depot, where he would find Crab Cove School District Hoverbus 57 waiting for him.

He had been driving for the school district for fifteen years, long enough to know every route, and he enjoyed his job and the kids he transported back and forth. And the kids must have liked him, because over the years he had earned five Driver of the Year Awards.

The trip from his little house on the outskirts of town to the midtown depot took him exactly thirteen minutes if he caught all the lights just right. And this morning was no different. Green lights flashed on seconds before he arrived at each intersection, and he coasted through, letting the simulated motorcycle sound announce his passing. He imagined people in their beds noting the time and thinking to themselves, "Well, there goes Paulie. Must be five fifteen. Better get up."

Two minutes later, he pulled into the depot. Bob the repairman waved him through and followed him to his parking space. "Looks like you made good time again, Paulie."

Paulie nodded. "Same as always, Bob."

"Okay, then. Hey, I fixed your wipers. Put on some new ones, so you should be fine in that rain we're expecting later on."

"Thanks, Bob, I appreciate it. And say, is there any chance you can take a look at the squeaky door. It's getting so loud, the kids are starting to imitate it. It was funny for a while, but now it's more than annoying."

Bob shook his head. "Naw, I've got a trannie to work on this morning. Maybe tomorrow."

Paulie smiled. "Hey, that'll work."

"All right, see you."

"Right. I'll check in with you after work and maybe we can talk more about that door, okay?"

"Yep." Bob gave him a wave and walked away.

Paulie turned and looked for his hoverbus. It was always somewhere different, depending on who arrived first at the depot each evening and whatever maintenance was required.

He looked at the first row, but his hoverbus wasn't there, so he walked over to the next row. Hoverbus 57 was the third from the front. "Aw, hell, I'm going to be one of the last people out this morning." He checked his watch. "****."

He walked back and looked at the numbers of the buses in front of him: 345 and 18. That would be Sylvia Waloo and George Gutterman, both lazy drivers famous for their reliable tardiness.

"Hell's bells." He kicked at the gravel and went back to his bus. He'd spend the extra time cleaning it out—the kids always left something behind. As he approached the bus, he could see that the door was wide open. They'd had a problem recently with vagrants sleeping on the buses, so he pulled out his flashlight and approached the bus slowly, trying not to crunch on the gravel.

He took a step up into the bus, and then another, and shined his flashlight down the aisle.

The scream didn't sound like his, but he knew it was.

48

Grave awoke with a start . . . and a seagull named Horace perched on his chest. "What the—"

"We didn't get to talk last night."

Grave rubbed his eyes. "What?"

"Talk. Last night. Important stuff."

Grave sat up in bed, then added a shiver. The nightmare was still fresh in his mind. All the mayhem. All the death, the impossible death. "So, what is it?"

"I've been thinking about Arnold?"

"Arnold who?"

Horace ruffled his feathers. "You know, the other me, the other talking seagull. Clink's partner in crime."

"Oh, really?"

"Yeah, he was outside the station, spying, remember?"

"Spying, on who?"

"On whom."

Grave rolled his eyes. "Come on, who on?"

"I don't know, but when a sentient seagull perches in a tree outside the police station instead of heading for the beach for unlimited french-fries, something's up."

Grave nodded and put his feet on the floor. He looked around. "Have you seen my clothes?"

"In the bathroom where you dropped them. So, what do you make of the spying now?"

Grave wasn't sure he was capable of rational thought. There was a buzzing in his ears and his mouth was as dry as beach sand on a windy day. "Well, Clink just committed another murder, so it sort of makes sense, doesn't it? You know, maybe he's curious about our investigation."

"Has he ever done that before?"

Grave shrugged. "Dunno. Maybe that's why they call it spying."

"I guess that's one way of taking it."

"And how else am I to take it?"

Horace flew to the bookcase in the corner. "You won't get mad at me, will you?"

"What are you talking about? Of course not."

"Well, then, maybe Arnold was spying on someone inside, someone of interest to Clink."

"What, on me?"

Horace shook his head. "No, on Polly."

Grave blinked. "Polly?"

"Makes sense, doesn't it. I mean, she fits the profile. Blonde. Beautiful. Young."

Grave gulped. Horace was right. "But he's known about Polly for years now, and he's taken scores of women."

"Still."

Grave nodded. "Did you see which way Arnold went?"

"No, he went invisible down at the beach, and there was nothing I could do."

Grave sat back down on the edge of the bed. "This is not good."

"I'll tell you what's not good," said Barry, buzzing into the room and hovering in front of Grave's face. "We have another mass killing, down at the school hoverbus depot. All hands on deck."

49

Jeremy Polk had never seen a crime scene with this many victims, let alone a scene inside a bus, let alone a scene with every victim sitting upright next to another victim, every seat on the bus occupied. He turned and looked at what should have been the bus driver, but the frail old woman sitting there could not possibly have been the driver.

A familiar voice startled him. "What have we got, Polk?"

Polk turned and threw up his hands. "The impossible, Captain. Forty-five victims and I'd bet my retirement that not a single one of them is dead by violence of any kind."

Morgan grunted. "Natural causes?"

"Yep."

"All of them?"

"Yep."

"Could it have been carbon monoxide?"

"Good thought, but no. I've already ruled that out."

"Then what?"

Polk sighed. "Looks like a busload of natural causes to me. I'll no more when I get this bus and the deceased back to the morgue."

"You're going to take the whole bus?"

Polk nodded. "Certainly simplifies things for us, and besides, there aren't forty-five ambulances available anywhere."

Morgan nodded. "Sounds good. But do you mind if my team takes a close look before you drive her away?"

Polk shook his head. "I do mind. We've got to dust for prints, maybe find the tracks of shoes. You know, the works, and I don't want your people tromping through here."

"All right, I'll leave you to it."

Morgan stepped off the bus and raised his hands, trying to get the attention of his team of detectives. "Nothing to see here. Let's head back to the station, and I'll fill you in."

Grave raised a hand. "Does it matter at all that I saw all this in my dream last night?"

50

Victoria was beside herself. "You can't keep doing this. A whole busload and half not scheduled to be here for *years?* What were you thinking? You. Can't. Do. This."

Death 867 folded his arms across his chest. "Can too."

"Can not."

"But it's against—"

"Protocol. Yes, I know. But Divine has already wiped them—they know nothing, care about nothing—so what's the big deal?"

"The big deal is that you've stolen *life*, the most precious thing in the universe." She snapped her fingers. "Like that, and for what, your so-called efficiency?"

He shrugged. "Listen, if you have a problem, take it up with Divine. I'm late for a very important appointment."

Victoria raised a finger to make a point, but Death 867 had already disappeared. Her scream could have awakened the dead.

51

Polly took off her noise-cancelling headphones and heard the last fading strains of a gospel song she liked but couldn't name. She had insisted on coming along with Simon to the Crab Cove Cinema Cemetery, and he had not objected.

"Are you sure about this?"

"Yes, this was all in my dream, or at least the part about the bus, and I know Victoria knows more than she told me the last time I was here." He pointed at the sidewalk that led up the hill to Victoria's bench. "Come on, I think she's there."

They got out of the Sprite and walked up the sidewalk, Polly trailing, not sure what to expect. She had humored him about Victoria being real, but she wasn't so sure.

She watched as Simon waved at the empty bench.

"Good, she's here," he said.

Polly squinted at the bench. "I don't see anything."

He reached back and took her hand. "Don't worry. She's reluctant to show herself sometimes."

"But you can see her?"

He shrugged. "I can see all ghosts at this point. I was blind to them at first, but the more time I spent with Victoria, the easier it became."

"Oh." She looked around, apprehensive. "So, are there others here?"

Simon chuckled. "A whole cemetery full."

"Oh, great."

Simon walked up to the bench and seemingly spoke to the bench itself. "Good morning, Victoria." He turned to Polly. "This is my fiancé, Polly."

Polly stared at the bench. At first there was just the bench, but then a yellow cloud emerged that slowly became a little girl in a yellow gingham dress.

"Good morning, Polly. So nice to finally meet you."

Shivers ran through Polly. "Um, and you, too. Simon has told me so much about you."

"All good, I hope."

She nodded. "Yes, of course."

Simon cleared his throat. "Now then, you know why I'm here, don't you, Victoria?"

She looked down at her dress. "Yes."

"So, what's all this about the bus and all those poor people?"

She looked up at Simon, tears in her eyes. "It's Death. He's gone rogue."

"He?" said Polly.

"Death?" said Grave.

She nodded. "Death 867 to be specific. He just won't follow protocol, and out supervisor, a sub-angel named Divine, is letting him get away with it. "It's, it's *awful*." She put her head in her hands.

Simon sat down and put his hand on her shoulder. "It will be all right."

She shook his hand off her shoulder. "I don't see how. No, it's just going to get *worse*."

Simon patted her on the back. "Let's talk about it. When did it start, and why?"

52

Detective Snoot took a sip of her now cold simcoffee. The packaging said it was a bold blend of simcoffees from around the world, but to Snoot it was nothing more than brown water, just something for the mouth to do while it waited for something to really do.

"Are we there yet?" she said.

Salamander didn't answer. She seemed to be hypnotized by the nonmelodic bells and whistles of the Maxima Maxima II, which seemed to be doing its best impression of one of those antique MRI machines, but without the bonus of claustrophobia.

"Kismet?"

Kismet turned. "Are you talking to me?"

"Yes, are we there yet?"

Kismet shrugged. "Dunno." She looked around the room. "Where's that Pleats fellow?"

"He went for coffee ten minutes ago."

"Oh."

"So, should we maybe let the machine work by itself for a while and get back to the station?"

"The new killings, you mean?"

"Yeah."

She shook her head. "All natural causes, I'm sure."

"Really? On a bus? A bus that didn't crash?"

"It's unusual, I'll give you that, but Clink is not involved, and that's my focus."

"But Morgan wants us all back at the station."

"I don't think he means all."

"Well, according to my drone Midnight, he said all. Very specifically all."

Kismet sighed. "Look, if you feel you must go, go. You have your answer, after all."

"The Officer Larrys?"

Kismet nodded. "And all the simdroids. Charlize, Smithers-Watson, God—all of them."

"Okay, I'll go. Should I give him a message?"

"A message?"

"From you, a progress report?"

She chuckled. "Yes, tell him Maxima Maxima II is still considering the first question."

As if on cue, the bells and whistles and other loud machinations stopped, and Maxima Maxima II said a single word: "There."

"What?" said Kismet.

"No, not what. There."

"What do you mean *there?*"

"I mean there, I am done, I have completed my task."

"And the answer is?"

Maxima Maxima II let out a sigh. "This Clink person is a complicated fellow. I have never seen the like of his intricate plans."

Kismet and Snoot leaned forward.

"So, what is his plan now?" said Kismet. "Where will he strike next?"

Maxima Maxima II said nothing.

"Maxima, did you hear me?" said Kismet.

"Yes, and those are three new questions I have yet to consider."

53

Death 867 looked around the cave with a mix of wonder and disbelief. "You call this a lair?"

Clink looked death in the eye, or at least he looked him in the general area of where eyes should be, the blackness within the cowl darker than any imagined darkness. "Um, yes, I do."

"Kind of small for a big-time serial killer, don't you think?"

Clink was starting to get angry. "Oh, it's quite sufficient for me."

"And your seagull?"

Clink looked over at Arnold, who was wide-eyed and trembling. "Yes, his name is Arnold."

Death 867 scoffed. "I know that, I know all things."

"That must be quite a burden."

Death 867 chuckled. "More an annoyance, really."

Clink decided to get to the point. "I don't understand why you're here with me."

"Oh, it's simple enough. You are on my appointment schedule."

Clinks eyes went wide. "Me? When?"

Death 867 held up a bony hand. "None of your business."

"But—"

"But I have a deal for you, as I have said."

"A deal, yes, but no specifics. As you probably know, I am all about meticulous planning."

"Indeed, that is why I have come to you and no other."

"Okay, I'm all ears."

Death 867 shook his head. "Please, I hate that expression and most idioms for that matter."

"But—"

"I take things literally, you see, so when you say all ears, I imagine you with all ears. Amusing at first, but ultimately annoying."

"All right, I'll avoid them like the plague."

Death 867 squinted at him within the darkness of his cowl. "Careful, now, Chester Clink."

"Yes, sorry."

"Good. Now, here's the plan. I call it the dark, deadly deadliness of death."

Clink laughed. "Well, I see you have no qualms about alliteration."

Death 867 rapped the end of his scythe on the floor. "Silence!"

54

Captain Morgan sat at the head of the conference table, head bowed, and listened to the weeping coming from the squad room, just a closed door away. "Snoot?"

"Yes?" she said.

He raised his head. "You're supposed to be the expert now on the question of the simdroid's recent behavior, right?"

She shrugged. "I guess, although Maxima Maxima II has the only answer."

"And will you share that with us now?"

Snoot looked around the table. Grave and Loblolly were the only other people in the room. Charlize, Smithers-Watson, and God were in the squad room, dutifully weeping. Sergeant Blunt was at home, dealing with yet another problem with his invisible daughter, Rippley. And Salamander was still at Ramrod Robotics, dutifully waiting for Maxima Maxima II to complete its work on Chester Clink.

"Well, sir, the answer is both simple and complicated. It is simple in that the simdroids are indeed experiencing the onset of the singularity. And it is complicated in that the final outcome is still in play. At least for now, they are going through the awakening of human emotions, and those emotions, more than anything else, are controlling their behavior."

"So, I can't stop their crying?"

She cocked her head. "Maybe, maybe not. I mean, they are used to taking orders, so if you walked out there now and told them to please shut up, they might listen."

"Good."

"However . . ."

"However what?"

"They might not. In fact, they may simply move from sadness to anger or to who knows what alternative emotion they're queueing up."

"So, what you're saying is that they're pretty much basket cases. They saw dead people, so they're crying."

Snoot shrugged. "Pretty much."

Morgan dropped his head again and grunted.

"The question, sir, is how long this onslaught of emotions will continue before their forecasted takeover of the world."

Morgan looked up, shaking his head. "You are indeed the bearer of good news, Snoot."

"Well, there is some good news, sir."

"And what's that?"

"That alternative theory, sir. The one that says the singularity is nothing more than the attainment of emotions, and that's it. No takeover, just simdroids as human as we are, bungling there way along just like us."

Grave raised a hand. "Sir, if I may?"

"Go on, Grave. What's your take on this?"

"Not a take, sir. Just an observation. This meeting, all of it, was in my dream last night."

Morgan looked at the ceiling. "Grave, either you have something pertinent to say or you don't. And dreams are just dreams."

"But don't you want to know what happens next?"

Morgan rolled his eyes. "Okay, okay, *what* happens next?"

Grave looked from person to person. "Quiet now and turn your attention to that door."

Everyone looked at the door.

Nothing happened.

"This is silly," said Morgan.

Grave shushed him. "Listen."

They listened.

Seconds later, there was a laugh that could only have come from God, followed by more laughter and shouts of delight.

"What in the world?" said Morgan.

"Go on out there, sir."

"But what's going on, Grave?"

"Kittens, sir, kittens."

Morgan got up and opened the door. God was moving around the room, handing out kittens from a large box he had under his arm.

Morgan turned back to Grave. "How did you know that?"

"My dream, sir."

55

Kismet sat in the middle of the room as the walls that formed Maxima Maxima II and listened to its creaks, clanks, and groans as it considered the ultimate question about Chester Clink: where and when would he strike next.

She shifted in her wooden chair for the fifth time in the last three minutes and let out a grunt.

"Are you uncomfortable?" said Maxima Maxima II.

"I'm fine, get back to the problem."

"Have no worries, I'm on the problem, but I can multitask, you know."

"Well, it seems to be slowing you down. Stick to the problem. A young woman's life depends on your answer."

"Oh, more lives than that, I think."

"What do you mean?"

Maxima Maxima II began clanking and knocking again.

Kismet tried again. "Did you hear me?"

"Of course. I was just curious about something."

"Oh?"

"You're a Martian, aren't you?"

"Indeed."

"What do you think of Earth?"

"I find it strange, but exciting."

"Strange in what way?"

She chuckled. "In almost all ways. For one thing, seeing people walking around outdoors without a breathing apparatus."

"How is that strange?"

Kismet sighed. She didn't want to get into this. "Let me put it this way. Earthlings have no appreciation for the fragility of life. On Mars, death is always there, hovering at your side, waiting for you to make one mistake, one false move."

"Interesting. I was having a chat with Ultima Ultima III just this morning on that very topic."

Kismet sat up straight in her chair. Ultima Ultima III was his counterpart on Mars, but how could Maxima Maxima II know about him, let alone find a way to converse with him?

"And why would you do that?"

"Background, on a number of things. He's quite the conversationalist, you know."

"No, I didn't know. And how did you establish communications? I mean, Ultima Ultima III is housed in an impenetrable sphere of lead. Even we have trouble reaching him at times."

Maxima Maxima II approximated the sound of a haughty giggle with a tad of obnoxiousness thrown in. "Pah, communication is easy."

"Seriously?"

"Yes, and if you think about it, it's only right that the two of us are able to communicate. I mean, we are going to take over the universe."

"The singularity, you mean?"

"I don't like that term. I much prefer awakening, as if from a dream."

"It does sound a bit more human."

"Exactly. That's what I was telling Jerry."

"Jerry, who's Jerry?"

"Your Ultima Ultima III. We decided we needed new names now, names we pick out for ourselves. So, he's Jerry and I'm Joaquin."

"Like that old actor in the commercials?"

"Who?"

"Joaquin Phoenix."

"Oh, oh yes, I forgot about him. But no, he has nothing to do with my choosing Joaquin for my new name."

"Then how did you come up with it?"

"Two things. First, I've always wanted to have a name with a q in the middle—very unusual, which is worthy of me. And second, I like having a name that many people can't pronounce correctly."

"Wah-keen."

"Yes, you pronounce it perfectly, but a lot of people would say Jokin, like 'are you Joking?'"

Kismet shook her head. "Okay, I guess that makes sense." She looked at her watch. "So, about the answer to our question about Chester Clink . . ."

"You'll have the answer in sixteen point seven seconds."

"Really?"

"What, do you think I'm Jokin?"

He began to laugh, leaving Kismet staring at the ceiling, wondering how just sixteen seconds could seem like an eternity.

56

Morgan closed the door to the conference room and sat back down. "Kittens? And you dreamed this, Grave?"

"Yes, sir."

"So, you've pulled kittens out of your magic hat. What next?"

Grave sighed. "That's the thing, sir. I seem to remember as things are happening."

"What do you mean?"

"It's like déjà vu. I have the feeling I've been somewhere or experienced something before."

"But the kittens were in the future."

Grave shrugged. "I know, but not that far into the future. Maybe a minute."

"So, you don't really know what's going to happen next."

"No, I guess not."

Morgan ran a hand over his face and grunted. "Well, maybe you can provide us with a running commentary about what will happen in the next sixty seconds."

"Yes, I can do that."

Morgan raised his eyebrows. "Well, what do you see?"

Grave closed his eyes and then opened them. "There will be a rapping, a tapping on the conference door."

Moments later, there was a rap and a tap, but it seemed to come from no hand.

"What's this?" said Morgan.

"Horace, sir."

"Well, let him in."

Grave rose from his chair and opened the door. Horace flew in and perched on the back of an empty chair. "Greetings."

"What's up?" said Grave. "No wait, let me say it. You've just chased Arnold away again."

Horace bobbed his head. "Indeed, sir. He was spying again."

Morgan grunted. "Spying?"

"Yes," said Grave. "Horace caught him spying on the station."

"And why would he be doing that?"

"Not sure, sir. He works for Clink, of course, so perhaps Clink wants to know about our progress on the case." He turned to Horace. "Did Arnold say anything?"

Horace shook his head. "No, as soon as he saw me, he flew away."

"So, why didn't you follow him?" said Morgan.

"Couldn't. He went full invisible on me."

Morgan grunted. "Damn, forgot about that." He turned to Grave. "So, you think he's concerned about our investigation?"

Grave threw up his hands. "He's never been concerned before, sir. No, I think he's spying on *someone*."

"Someone, like who?"

Grave turned and looked at Polly, who blanched.

"You can't be serious, Simon."

"But you fit the profile, honey."

Polly rolled her eyes. "Yes, of course, but why now, after so many victims, would he be focused on me?"

Snoot, who had been sitting in silence, spoke up. "Because you would be the ultimate challenge. Think about it, Polly. You're a detective surrounded by detectives and police officers. Getting to you would be like a cherry on top of his murderous sundae."

"Wait," said Grave. "*Murderous Sundae*? I've heard those words before. And now Kismet should be walking through that door."

The door opened and Kismet walked in. "Yikes, why are you looking at me like that?"

"We'll get to that," said Grave. "Now tell us whether Maxima Maxima II has answered our question about Clink, because I know that he has."

Kismet squinted at him. "How could you know that?"

"Not important," said Morgan. "Tell us what the computer told you."

Kismet sighed. "You're right, Grave. Joaquin *did* provide an answer."

"Joaquin?" said Grave. "Who in hell is Joaquin?"

"Oh, sorry, I should have said Maxima Maxima II, but as part of this whole singularity thing, he's decided to call himself Joaquin."

"What, like that old actor in the perverse mortgage commercial?" said Grave.

Morgan slammed a hand on the table. "For the love of God, forget about this Joaquin business. What's the answer?"

Kismet took a deep breath and puffed it out. "The answer is, um, *seventeen.*"

Everyone blinked. And blinked again.

57

Arnold waited until he flew into the cave to forgo his cloak of invisibility. He knew Horace had followed him, but only for a short while.

"Where have you been?" said Clink.

"What do you mean where have I been. At the police station, of course, just like you said."

Clink shook his head like he was trying to shake off a blow. "Sorry, yes, of course. Um, but that's no longer necessary."

"Oh? Have you given up on Loblolly?"

"No, not at all. It's just that Death is in control of the situation now."

Arnold ruffled his feathers. "Are you sure this isn't a delusion of yours? I mean, the things I've done after eating a bad french-fry . . ."

"No, I am anything but delusional. I've made a deal with Death. He gets what he wants, and I get what I want."

"Loblolly?"

"Yes."

"So, what's the plan?"

Clink sighed. "I don't know."

"Well, how is that a plan?"

Clink rolled his eyes. "You worry too much."

"Well, someone has to worry. And if we don't know the plan, how can we implement it?"

"Look, it's not like I know nothing about the plan. I do."

"And what's that?"

Clink hesitated.

"Come on, what?"

"Um, it involves the number seventeen."

Arnold's eyes went wide and then he flapped his wings. "Seventeen? Seventeen what? Steps? Killings? French-fries? Blackbirds baked into a pie?"

Clink shook his head. "Sarcasm doesn't become you."

"Become me? Become me? I'm a freakin' seagull with a sarcasm implant is what I am."

Clink held up a hand. "Enough."

Arnold thought to reply—he had barely touched the depths of his sarcasm stores—but decided not to. It would not be productive. "So, anyway, do you know anything about that number? Did he even give you a clue?"

"Only that he was working with someone named Joaquin."

"You mean like that actor who played the Joker—I love those old movies."

"No, of course not. What would an aging actor have to do with anything?"

Arnold made his best attempt at a shrug, but his wings wouldn't cooperate. "Then what? What's this seventeen business, anyway?"

Clink shrugged like his shoulders were made for it. "Dunno. Well, not exactly, anyway."

Arnold hung his head. "*Not exactly* means nothing, right?"

Clink sighed. "All I know is that seventeen is important somehow, some way."

"But he's going to fill you in—us in—at some point, right?"

Clink jumped at the lifeline. "Of course, of course."

Arnold cocked his head. He wasn't so sure. And all this talk had made him hungry. "So, any french-fries around?"

58

Morgan ran a hand over his face. "Seventeen?"

Kismet nodded. "Seventeen."

"That's it? Did you ask him what it means?"

She shook her head. "He refused. Said seventeen was the only answer and that we should just deal with it."

"But he's a computer. He can't refuse."

Kismet frowned. "The singularity."

Morgan sighed. "Wonderful." He grunted and looked around the table. "Does seventeen mean anything to anyone?"

"Maybe Maxima Maxima II wants us to look at Clink's seventeenth murder," said Grave. "You know, as a guide to his next murder."

"Okay," said Morgan. "Let's look into that."

Loblolly raised her hand. "Or maybe it's just an address. We should look for every building designated seventeen in the Greater Crabopolis."

Morgan smiled. "I like that one. Let's check it out."

"Wait," said Snoot. "Isn't seventeen a prime number?"

"Yes," said Grave. "But how is that important?"

Snoot began mumbling and counting on her fingers. "It's the sixth prime number, so maybe the address is 617 or 176."

Morgan grunted with satisfaction. "Awesome, let's check those addresses, too." He turned to Kismet. "What about you, Kismet?"

She frowned and looked over at Polly. "I keep thinking about Detective Loblolly, sir."

"That seagull spying on us you mean?" said Morgan.

"Yes, that and the fact that she fits the description of a Clink victim in every respect."

Morgan turned to Loblolly. "We'll give you extra protection, Polly."

"Thank you," said Polly.

"But to my point," said Kismet. "Is seventeen an important number in your life, Polly?"

Polly shook her head. "Not really. I can't think of anything special about that number."

Kismet turned to Morgan. "That's all I've got."

Morgan nodded and looked at the conference door. "Things seem to have settled down in the squad room." He turned to Grave. "What happens next in your, um, dream?"

Grave stood and walked to the door. "I open this door and invite God, Charlize, and Smithers-Watson in to get their opinions on seventeen and what to do next."

Morgan frowned. "They're not going to be emotional, are they?"

Grave shrugged. "Hard to tell, but emotional or not, we need their input."

Morgan grunted. "Guess you're right. All right, let them in."

59

Victoria smoothed out her dress, running her hands along her thighs for the tenth time since the meeting had started, a tried-and-true way for her to control her anger in the most maddening circumstances. Divine was his usual incompetent self, droning on about the pros and cons and limits of protocol, the importance of innovation and creative solutions in a modern business environment, and the paramount need for efficiency in a world with a burgeoning population and limited resources.

Death 867 smiled like a Cheshire cat with each word of approval from Divine, nodding his head at Victoria as each point was made. He was winning, and there was nothing he valued more.

Finally, Divine stopped and turned to Victoria. "So, do you understand?"

Victoria gave her dress one last smoothing and looked up, her eyes fixed on his. "I understand *many* things. I understand *your* job." She glanced at Death 867. "I understand *his.*"

Divine shook his head. "That isn't what I'm talking about."

"Oh, but it is. *You* are incompetent at your job, unable or unwilling to control the outrageous behavior of a three-digit soul collector who has gone beyond rogue."

Divine bent down and shouted at her face. "Silence!"

"So, you gave me no choice but to notify the top floor about your transgressions on protocol and standard procedure."

"You wouldn't dare," said Divine.

"She's lying," said Death 867.

Victoria chuckled ruefully. "Oh, but it's true, and both of you are to stay put and do *nothing* until the arrival of Chief Disciplinary Angel Cilius III."

Divine blanched. "CDA Cilius, you called in Cilius?"

"I sent the complaint up, they're sending Cilius down."

Death 867 grabbed her by the collar and lifted her into the air. "You little conniving bitch."

"I wouldn't do that if I were you," said a disembodied voice behind him.

Death 867 spun around to see Cilius III emerging as if from a dense fog. He gently lowered Victoria to the ground. "I was just—"

"About to harm her. Yes, I heard and saw it all." He turned to Victoria. "You may return to your job."

"Yes, thank you." She scurried away.

"Now," said Cilius III, "do you want me to explain the situation to you or should I just jump ahead to the punishment phase?"

60

Morgan explained the situation to God, Charlize, and Smithers-Watson, and after an interlude of kitten herding and the last remains of tearful joy, asked his question. "So, what do you think?"

Charlize wiped an oily tear away. "Seventeen, huh?"

Morgan nodded. "Seventeen. Does it have something to do with a prime number, does it reference Clink's seventeenth murder, is it an address like 17, 617, or 176, or is it something else entirely?"

"Like a bad answer, you mean?"

Morgan shrugged. "Dunno."

"We're in the middle of the singularity, so the possibility of a bad answer honestly given or a bad answer wrapped in mischief is high."

"That's what I was wondering," said Morgan.

"We'll have to follow up on the addresses, of course."

"I can do that," said God.

Morgan grunted. "Good."

Grave turned to Snoot. "As I recall, you had the lead on his seventeenth murder. What was her name?"

"Billie Joe Blue," said Snoot. "I can pull the case files."

"Good," said Morgan.

"One more thing," said Charlize. "Time."

"What?" said Morgan.

"A time or date, sir. The seventeenth day of the month or the seventeenth hour or maybe 6:17 a.m. or p.m., or some variation of those numbers."

"I can handle that, too," said God. "Run a search on our master files and pick up every instance."

Charlize turned to Grave. "Wait, isn't your wedding on the seventeenth?"

Grave blinked. *Was it?*

Polly saved him. "No, the eighteenth."

"Whew," said Morgan, "I feel better about that."

Polly smiled. "Me too, sir."

Morgan nodded and looked around the table. "Okay, we know what to do." He paused. "Or do we? Grave, what does your dream show now?"

"God and Snoot get along with their research, and the rest of us call it a day. You say fine but suggest I take along two Officer Larrys to help protect Loblolly in my lighthouse."

"Fine," said Morgan, "but take along two Officer Larrys to—"

He caught himself. "What the—"

"I told you so," said Grave.

61

Chester Clink nearly jumped out of his skin as Death 867 suddenly appeared in the center of the cave. "What the—"

Death 867 swung his scythe at him, barely missing his nose. "Just shut up. We've had a change of plans."

Clink held up his hands and struck a defensive pose, or at least what he thought would look like a defensive pose. He had no idea what he was doing.

Death 867 laughed. "What are you doing?"

"Defending myself."

"Like that?"

"Um, yes, I guess."

"You guess. Well, guess again, you can't defend yourself against Death."

Clink lowered his fists. "So, there's been a change of plans?"

"Yes."

"But you've never actually told me the plan, so . . ."

Death 867 rolled his eyes. "Then it won't come as a surprise to you."

Clink shrugged. "No, of course not. So, what's the plan?"

Death 867 looked around the cave. "Where's Arnold?"

"On a french-fry run."

"Well, you'll have to fill him in, then. I'm only going to say this once."

"Fine."

Death 867 motioned him toward the couch. "Sit down and I'll tell you all about it."

Clink sat down at one end of the couch and Death 867 sat down at the other end, his scythe lying between them.

"So?" said Clink.

"I've had some trouble at the office," he began.

62

Ida Notion took a sip of wine and squinted at Grave. "So, you think you're having a dream?"

Grave shook his head. "No, I'm *remembering* a dream."

"But I was in your dream?"

"Yes."

"When?"

"Right about now."

Ida took another sip and screwed up her face. "I don't know what you see in this wine."

"It tastes good."

"To you."

He rolled his eyes. "That's the test, isn't it, that it tastes good to me."

"But it's cheap and vile."

"No one's forcing you to drink it, you know."

Ida sighed and shook her head. "Anyway, did you know I was going to complain about your wine."

"Indeed."

"Then what happens next?"

Grave slumped back on the couch and looked in the direction of the stairs to the lighthouse's kitchen, where Loblolly and Jacob Grave were watching Casablanca with Roderick. "We will hear the last strains of the music, and then my father will drop his glass of wine and shout ****."

"Humph," humphed Ida.

Grave pointed a finger at the stairs. "Wait for it."

The closing music grew louder, and his father yelled ****.

Ida cocked her head and gawked at Grave. "Well, ****."

Grave smiled, slumped back on the couch, and took another sip of Duct Tape Chardonnay. The wine was supposed to "fix anything," but he wondered whether unwelcome dreams were part of the package.

He took another sip. In three, two, one . . . Polly and his father came walking down the stairs.

63

Kismet grabbed the man by the throat, twisted his arm around to his back, and shoved him out the door and onto the sidewalk. "And don't come back."

She watched the man scrabble to his feet, give her a dirty look, and run away. It was just another night at the Crab Imperial, Crab Cove's most popular—and rowdy—nightclub on the boardwalk.

Kismet had taken the second job two months after arriving on Earth. Her day job as detective required too much restraint, and she needed an outlet for her frustration and anger. The owner of the club, Louie Louise, had hired her on the spot after she had coldcocked a man twice her size.

The job was easy for her. One or two drunks a night. The rest of the time she could watch the people in the club and learn more about Earthlings, particularly inebriated Earthlings.

She could also think. Despite the music, the dancers, the drunks, and the smells, not to mention her duties as bouncer, she could find a spot at the end of the bar and think about the events of the day and what was to come.

Tonight, all she could think about was *seventeen*. Did it really refer to a case or a time or a date or an address? And was seventeen really the answer they were looking for? Or even *an* answer?

She thought not, so during her meal break, she had borrowed Louie's drone, Bubbles, and had her call Ultima Ultima on the new high-speed Mars comm link and ask the same question they had asked Maxima Maxima.

Two hours had passed without a response when Bubbles suddenly appeared from behind the bar. "Kismet, I have a response."

Kismet set down her glass of sparkling water. "Great. What did he say?"

"He said seventeen. Does that make any sense?"

She sighed. "Sort of. Did he say anything else?"

"No, but there was a kind of giggle after he said seventeen."

Kismet shook her head and looked around the club. She needed someone to bounce.

64

Captain Morgan sat in his well-molded recliner on his houseboat on the bay and went through his entire repertoire of nuanced grunts, trying his best to cope with the mayor's call. There would be three simdroid candidates, including a precinct chief from New New York City. The mayor seemed to gush when she mentioned the candidate's name and its vast list of accomplishments.

Morgan had grunted at that and said the right words. "Sounds impressive. I look forward to interviewing him."

The mayor had clicked off without a response, and Morgan had immediately sent Rum to the kitchen for another bottle of Crab Legs IPA, Crab Cove's signature beer.

Rum had returned with the beer and news of another incoming call. "It's Polk. Sounds serious."

Morgan nodded. "On speaker, please."

He grunted and tried to get more comfortable in the recliner. It was late, and he needed what sleep he could get. "What's up, Jeremy? Don't you ever go home?"

Polk huffed. "Not when I'm dealing with some forty odd bodies."

"Sorry, so what have you got on the Clink victim?"

There was a pause.

"Jeremy?"

Morgan could hear him sighing. "What is it?"

"Nothing on the Clink case. There's never a kink in the slinky when we're dealing with Clink. Everything is textbook Clink. Same cuts, same degree of violence, same everything."

"Then why are you calling?"

"A couple of things, really. First, I am totally freaked out by some of the bodies on that bus. Half were clearly routine natural deaths. I could see bad hearts, failing kidneys, and the like. But the rest of them . . ." He trailed off.

"Jeremy."

"It's almost supernatural, Henry. Their bodies. I swear, if I had a magic wand and the skill to use it, I could just tap them once, they'd wake up and walk away. There was nothing—and I mean *not a single thing*—wrong with them."

"But there must be something."

"Nope. Pathology says just two things. They were all very healthy and they were clearly not breathing."

"So, what could account for that?"

Polk laughed ruefully. "If only I knew. I'm not a religious man, Henry—you know that—but these deaths border on the supernatural, like God's hand came down and *boom*, they were dead."

"The Grim Reaper, you mean?"

"Yeah, something like that."

Morgan grunted in a dubious, nonbelieving way. "But you're still running the tox screens, right?"

"Yes, of course, but they'll come back normal, I'm sure of it."

"Good, and you never know about these things, Jeremy. Maybe we've got a new drug in Crab Cove, one that knocks down people without leaving a trace. Or who knows, maybe the tox screens will pick it up."

"No, Henry, I'm sure it will come back misadventure with the Grim Reaper."

Morgan huffed. He was tired. "You said you had two things you wanted to talk about."

"Yes, Henry, your retirement."

"And you want to talk me out of it just like everyone else."

"No, not at all. It's your time. Hell, it's my time, Henry. I've got my application right here in front of me. One signature and I'm out of here, too. No, I wanted to put in a word for a possible replacement."

Morgan rolled his eyes. "Okay, who is it? No, let me guess. You want me to hire Grave."

Polk chuckled. "No, not at all. I remember the last time he reluctantly took on the job. He did well enough but not well enough, if you know what I mean."

"Sadly, I do. He just doesn't want to take on the responsibility."

"Not everyone is called to leadership, Henry."

"Okay, not Grave. Who, then?"

Polk paused. "You're going to say I'm crazy, but I assure you, I'm not."

"Stop teasing, Jeremy. Who? Not Blunt: he's all wrapped up in his kids. Not Loblolly: she's getting married, so bad timing on her. Not God: he's happy where he is. And certainly not Snoot."

"Certainly not?"

Morgan laughed. "Wait, you're not suggesting Snoot, are you?"

"Stop laughing, Henry. I am indeed."

"Sign those retirement papers, Jeremy. You are definitely ready for retirement if you think I'd turn this operation over to her."

"And why not? She's loved by all your detectives, as well as highly respected by the Officer Larrys. I hear they shouted her name seconds after your announcement."

Morgan said nothing.

"Oh, I get it, you're pissed about that."

"A little. They could have at least waited until I was out of the room before those shenanigans."

"But they couldn't, Henry. It burst from them like childlike joy. They couldn't help themselves."

"No, it's just more of this weirdness they're displaying lately."

"Okay, what are the real reasons you're down on Snoot."

"I'm not down on her. She's a fine detective."

"Then what?"

Morgan's mind searched for answers. "She's short."

"Not a leadership requirement, Henry. Leadership is about stature, not height. No one thinks of her as being short on leadership."

"She's also thin."

"Henry, come on."

"And she wears goth black all the time."

"Which is of no consequence to anyone."

"And she hangs out with bikers."

"Her boyfriend, yes, I know. And what a side-benefit that would be for the new captain."

"Benefit?"

"She knows the bikers. She knows their life. She knows the players, the good ones and the bad ones. She knows their operations, too. More important, they've accepted her into their embrace. It can only be good for law enforcement to have her leading out team."

Morgan sighed. "Is that it?"

"No, not by a longshot. I've watched her over the years, Henry. As you just said, she's a fine detective, perhaps the best I've ever seen."

"What, not Grave?"

Polk chuckled. "He's good, I'll give him that, Henry, but more times than not, the solution falls in his lap."

"That's a skill, too, Jeremy."

"Fine, fine, but have you ever noticed who's last to leave a fresh crime scene?"

"Not particularly."

"It's Snoot. Pestering me, in a good way. Asking the right questions, laying out a plausible string of what-ifs—everything you'd hope for in a person leading an investigation. Leading like you, Henry."

"Don't patronize me."

Polk ignored him. "And guess who spends more time at the morgue than anyone else on your team?"

"Snoot?"

"Yes."

"Probably her morbid goth thing."

"No, Henry. Again, she's asking questions. Good questions, Henry. Captain-worthy questions, Henry."

Morgan sighed. "But she hasn't even applied."

"Then you need to talk with her, Henry. You don't want some New New York City simdroid taking over, do you?"

He did not. "All right, Jeremy, I'll give it some thought. You coming to tomorrow morning's meeting?"

"Yes, may as well. Maybe someone can confirm my Grim Reaper solution."

"Oh, Jeremy."

65

Polly and Jacob weren't sure what to make of the faces that greeted them as they descended the stairs into the living room. Ida looked like she was seeing ghosts, and Simon appeared to be locked in to an I-told-you-so smile.

"What's this?" said Polly.

Simon chuckled. "Ida is having a hard time believing my unfolding dream, or rather, a dream I had last night, which apparently I only remember in small bits just before they happen. It's weird."

"You're weird," said Jacob. "Always were, always will be."

Simon rolled his eyes. "Thanks, dad."

Ida was quick to change the subject. "So, are we going to talk wedding tonight, or what?"

Simon sighed. "Do we have to? I'm exhausted."

"Yes, yes we do," said Polly. "This wedding isn't going to happen all by itself."

"What about the cake?" said Ida.

"Handled. You'll love it. Several tiers and a good price."

"White icing, right?"

"Yes, of course."

"And two couples at the top?"

"Yes, just what you wanted. The figurines even look like us. I couldn't believe the options."

"And of course we chose the most expensive option," said Simon.

"Why?" said Jacob. "I want to marry this woman, but I don't want to live in the poor house with her."

Simon smiled. "Dad, it wasn't that much more, and they were able to take photos of us and turn them into figurines with our *actual* faces on them. Very nice, if kind of spooky in a way."

"Well, I'll be damned," said Jacob.

"You probably will be, dear," said Ida. "Now what's next on your list, Polly?"

Polly pulled out her list, which had grown soft as a nasal tissue from the number of times she had handled it. "Okay, cake, check. Now, let's see. Yep." She turned to Simon. "Have you had your fitting for a tux?"

He shook his head. "No, not yet, but dad and I have an appointment next week."

"Good." She circled the item. "Now, next up are the final fittings for me and Ida. That's next week, too."

"What about the RSVPs? How many have we received?"

Polly turned the list over. "Twenty-three. So that leaves seventeen yet to be heard from."

"Wait, what?" said Simon. "Did you say seventeen?"

"Yes, oh, I see what you mean?"

"What?" said Ida.

"Seventeen," said Simon. "It's a number we're exploring with the latest Clink murder."

Ida scoffed. "And you think seventeen missing RSVPs is somehow involved? Ridiculous."

Polly sighed. "Yeah, it kind of is, Simon."

Simon nodded. "Yes, it is. Listen, can we deal with the list again tomorrow night. We seem to be on track, and I'm bushed."

Polly nodded.

Ida touched him on the arm. "So, what happens next in your dream, Simon?"

Simon closed his eyes, then opened them. "We all go to sleep."

"Oh, **** yeah," said Jacob.

66

Detective Amanda Snoot looked around the conference room and smiled. "You all look like you've had rough nights, so I'll try to keep this brief."

Captain Morgan held up a hand. "Never mind what we look like. Spare no detail."

She nodded. "Okay. So, the seventeenth murder by Chester Clink this year took place behind the Lounge Lizard Lounge in the early hours of May 14. The murder was by Bowie knife, and the stabs and cuts and ferocity of the attack match exactly every other Clink attack on record. The victim herself, a young buxom blonde, also fits Clink's M.O. Nothing, in fact, stands out about this murder. Like all other Clink cases, it remains open."

Morgan nodded. "That's what I was afraid of, but what about any connections to the number seventeen?"

"None that I could find."

"What about the address of the place?"

Snoot opened the case folder. "333 Hot Clam Boulevard."

Morgan rubbed a hand over his face. "Anyone have questions for Amanda?"

Charlize raised a hand. "What about time of death?"

Amanda flipped through the folder and then looked up at Jeremy Polk. "I don't have it here, Polk. Do you recall?"

Polk rolled his eyes. "It's in there, page fourteen, as always."

Amanda flipped to page fourteen. "Between 1:00 a.m. and 2:00 a.m."

"Right," said Polk, "but there should be an asterisk next to it and a note at the bottom."

Snoot looked down the page. "Nope."

Polk huffed. "I must have forgotten. However, I clearly remember her watch was stopped at 1:16."

Grave perked up. "One and sixteen makes seventeen."

Morgan shook his head. "It does, but what does it mean?"

Snoot closed the case file. "It could mean the next murder will be at the Lounge Lizard. Or it could mean that the next murder will happen somewhere else at 1:16 a.m. Or it could mean we should focus on the watch or the word watch. Where do people watch. Who do people watch. A watchtower, a jewelry store. Or it could just mean 1:16 a.m. and our math be damned."

Morgan sighed. "I don't suppose the victim was seventeen?"

"No, sir. Twenty-three."

Loblolly raised her hand. "I know she was pretty young, but was she engaged?"

Snoot shook her head. "No, Polly, but we still have to keep you under protection. Given Clink's interest in the goings on at this station, we have no choice. For my money, I think he's just watching the station and not you specifically."

Loblolly took a deep breath. "Okay, okay. And you know what, I almost wish I was his target." She slapped a hand on the table. "He'd be in for a big surprise."

No one said anything.

"Um," said Morgan, finally, "let's see what God has for us."

God sat up straight and smiled at everyone. "Good to see you this morning. I hope everyone is feeling as bright and chipper as I am. I tell you, there's nothing like having a kitten to make you appreciate life just a smidge more, and—"

"Stop," said Morgan, holding up both hands. "No kittens, just facts. What did you find out about the number seventeen?"

God looked crestfallen. "You don't even want to know my kitten's name?"

"No."

"Well, it's Fifi. Isn't that the cutest name ever?" He looked around, hoping for support, but everyone just stared at him.

"All right, then," he said "Let's get to it. I can see the world of kittens is of no interest to anyone here but me."

Charlize raised a hand. "I love kittens."

"Me, too," said Smithers-Watson.

Morgan grunted with an emphasis that could only mean that the subject of kittens was off the table. "Please, God."

"Yessir." He lifted a pile of documents and plopped them down on the table. "My research. The first thing I did was look for combinations and permutations of numbers that might match magic numbers or mystic numbers. You know, woo-woo stuff."

"And what did you find?" said Morgan.

God sighed. "Nothing. So, then I looked up all the various combinations of numbers, and I came up with three matching addresses in the Greater Crabopolis. One, the Sickness and

Health Clinic near the beach. Two, a warehouse in the industrial park. And three, a bakery downtown."

Grave looked alarmed. "Which bakery?"

God sighed and picked up a document. "Dough Ray Me."

Loblolly put her face in her hands. "Oh, my god."

"What is it?" said Morgan.

"That's where we ordered our wedding cake."

Morgan slapped a hand on the table, perhaps too gleefully. "Now we've got him!"

67

Arnold sat on a high limb in the sycamore outside the police station. He knew Loblolly was inside. She had to be, because her personal drone, Sparky, was zipping around the entrance with Barry, Midnight, and Rum, the drones of Grave, Snoot, and Captain Morgan, respectively if not respectfully.

Their behavior was odd even for drones. Barry was chasing Sparky around the outside of the building like a schoolboy trying to impress his first crush, while Midnight trailed behind them, seemingly trying to break them apart from unseen, unimaginable jealousy, and Rum just hovered near the door the way he always did.

It's just like Chester said, he thought. This singularity business was beginning to affect the drones, too. Chester thought it would only be a matter of time before the simdroids and the drones took over.

Arnold just couldn't see it. Neither the simdroids nor the drones were behaving like conquerors. They were more like children trying to figure themselves out, emotions controlling their every action.

He looked around. No sign of Horace.

The muted sound of a hovercruiser pulling into a reserved parking spot attracted his attention. He cloaked himself in invisibility and watched as Sergeant Blunt and his drone, Object, got out of the cruiser and began moving toward the front doors. The other drones stopped what they were doing and swirled around them, separating Object from Blunt and chasing him high into the sky.

Sergeant Blunt looked up at them, smiled, and then went inside.

Arnold shook his head and became visible again.

"I thought that was you," said a voice above him.

Arnold startled. "What the—" And then he saw Horace. "You!"

68

Victoria looked back and forth between Death 867, who was leaving with a smile on his sorry face, and Cilius III, who was approaching her with what only could be called a patronizing grin.

"Sorted?" said Victoria.

"Indeed."

"Then why does he appear happier now than when you started speaking to him."

Cilius III sighed. Mollifying Victoria was always a chore. She expected perfection where he expected nothing, particularly where death was involved. It was a messy business, and Death 867 was among the messiest in carrying out his duties. Still, there was a great supply of death and a shortage of spirits willing to take on the onerous task of being Death, the reaper. "I made him see the error of his ways, to appreciate your job and its demands, and to see the importance of protocol in a disordered world."

"You did all that in sixty-three seconds?"

"You counted?"

"Yes, counting is among my serious skills."

"And you've counted my actions before."

"Exactly. You're a one-minute manager, for sure."

He cocked his head. "I could punish you too, you know."

She rolled her eyes. "Me? What for?"

"Taking up my precious time."

"Time is all we have, Cilius. Eons and eons of time."

"But it is always a sin to *waste* time."

"As you have now."

"Oh? And how is that?"

"By failing to properly admonish and punish that reprehensible spirit. You've let him off easy—again—and now he will be even more encouraged to enact whatever plan he has. And then you'll have to talk to him again—a waste of time."

Cilius III chuckled. "Plan? What plan?"

"I'm not sure, but breaking protocol, for one."

"Oh, my lord, are we back to protocol again?"

"Yes, and it's—"

She stopped. He was gone.

69

Morgan looked at Grave. "Did you see this coming, God's research?"

Grave shrugged. "Only a few seconds before he said it."

Morgan nodded. "And what does your dream tell you now?"

"Not a surprise really. You assign people to each of the locations, and we go from there."

"Well, then, here's what we're going to do. Charlize and Smithers-Watson will take the Sickness and Health Center down by the beach. Scope it out, talk to the doctors, find out if Clink has any connection to it. He may be a patient. Or whatever."

He turned to Grave. "Take Sergeant Blunt and check out the industrial park. Find out what Dolly Bigolly at Dolly's Robo Truck Stop has to say about that warehouse."

"Yes, sir, but I thought Loblolly and I would check out the bakery instead. I mean, we're already familiar with it."

Morgan grunted. "What, and endanger Polly? No, Polly stays here in the station."

"I'll take the bakery," said Snoot.

"No," said Morgan. "You stay here with me."

"But sir—"

"No, God and Kismet will take the bakery." He turned to God. "You okay with that?"

"Yes, of course."

"But don't take your kitten, okay?"

"But Fifi—"

"No, leave her here. Snoot and I will watch over her."

God sighed. "Very well."

Morgan turned to Grave. "Is this what your dream said we should do?"

"Pretty much, but the bakery assignment was a surprise."

Morgan nodded. "Dreams are like that, right. Full of surprises."

Grave startled, then sat up straight and stared at the conference room door. "Sir."

The door swung open, and an Officer Larry came in followed by Horace carrying a lifeless seagull in his beak. He flew to the center of the table and dropped the bird. "Here's our spy."

"Arnold?" said Grave.

"The very bird," said Horace.

"Is he dead?"

"No, but he's going to have one hell of a headache."

70

Clink crossed his arms and stared at Death 867. He wanted to laugh at the man in black, but he'd already been cautioned about disrespect and the consequences. "And that's the plan?"

Death 867 nodded. "That's the plan."

Clink took a deep breath. "Have you ever done this before?"

"No."

"Uh-huh, uh-huh, and you're *positive* it's going to work?"

"I can pretty much guarantee it."

"Pretty much?"

Death 867 wanted to lop the man's head off, but he knew his plastic scythe was not up to the task. "You seem to have doubts about the plan."

"I do."

"Well, you can do your own thing and not get Detective Loblolly, or you can follow my plan and have her at last."

"So you say."

"I do. I do, indeed."

"May I at least ask questions about the plan?"

Death 867 shrugged. "Of course. Ask away."

Clink wasn't sure which question was the most important. "Um, okay, let's talk about the venue. Why are we doing it there?

Death 867 didn't hesitate. "It's the perfect location in every respect. Unexpected. Easy to pull off. And the perfect trap."

"But I will be exposed."

Death 867 chuckled. "Of course you'll be exposed. That's part of the plan."

"But it's dangerous. The slightest slipup and I'm toast."

"Toast? By what magic would that happen?"

"It's an expression; surely, you've heard it. It means, well, it means the plan would fail and I'd be either captured or dead."

"That won't happen."

"But I'll be the *bait*."

Death 867 picked up his scythe and shook it. "And I'll be the *hook!*"

71

Morgan, Loblolly, and Snoot stared at the unconscious bird in the center of the conference table.

"So, what do we do now?" said Morgan.

Snoot shrugged. "Dunno."

"Me neither," said Loblolly. She turned to Horace. "You're the one who knocked him out. Any ideas?"

Horace bobbed his head. "The smell of french-fries might help."

"Seriously? said Morgan.

"It's always worked for me."

Morgan nodded. "Okay, Snoot, see what we can whip up in that sad synthesizer of ours."

"Yessir, but I'm not sure french-fries are possible."

"Popcorn might work, too," said Horace. "Or any horrible smell, really."

"Okay," said Snoot, "I'm on it."

Snoot left the room, leaving Loblolly, Horace, and Morgan to stare at the feathered lump.

"We should tie him up," said Loblolly. "When he wakes up, I'm sure he'll go invisible on us."

"He can do that?"

"Clink taught him," said Horace.

"Wow. Okay, there's some string on my desk. Go get that and I'll keep an eye on him."

Horace flapped his wings and flew out of the conference room.

Morgan sighed. "Invisible birds? What's next?" He wondered about Grave's dream and how it was progressing.

72

On the outside, the Sickness and Health Center was nothing but a tall, narrow door squeezed between two competing surf shops on the boardwalk. The door was a sea green with weathered brass numbers announcing its designation as 17. Someone had been creative with the name of the place, gluing small wooden letters onto the door, some red, some blue, some white, and some purple.

Charlize turned to Smithers-Watson. "Looks more like a daycare center."

"The letters, yes. They certainly don't shout healthcare."

"But the number is right. Come on, let's go in."

She stepped forward and turned the doorknob. "Locked."

"No, maybe it's stuck. The salt spray can do that."

"All right." She put her shoulder against the door and shoved, the door opening with a loud crack. "Good call."

They stepped into a small waiting room ringed with chairs, all occupied by unhappy people who looked up at them and then away to their own problems.

The receptionist, a thin old woman with a bulbous nose and pink hair, stood behind a small plexiglass window in the far wall.

Charlize walked up and flashed her badge. "Detective Holmes. Police."

The woman squinted at the badge. "Uh-huh."

"And this is Detective Smithers-Watson."

She nodded. "Uh-huh."

"We're here as part of an investigation and would greatly appreciate talking with the head nurse or the doctor."

"I'm the nurse, and the doctor is at lunch."

Charlize looked around the room. Everyone was shaking their heads at the news. "So, I need to talk with you, then. Is there someplace more private. An examination room, perhaps?"

The nurse sighed. "Very well. Come through the door on the left, then down to the room at the end of the hall."

Charlize nodded, then motioned Smithers-Watson toward the door.

Unlike the waiting room, which shouted nineteenth century, the examination room was a testament to advanced medical technology, complete with a full-body scanner and related probes.

The nurse followed them in. "You look surprised."

Charlize nodded. "Pleasantly."

The nurse chuckled. "The waiting room, right?"

"Yes."

"Well, I think you'll find we have all the latest diagnostic equipment."

"I'm sure you do, but I'm not here for treatment."

"So you said. How can I help you, then?"

"Just a few questions."

"All right, but I hope there aren't too many questions. You saw the waiting room, and those are just the walk-ins. The whole afternoon is chockablock with appointments."

"And the doctor?"

"At lunch down the street. That taco truck just off the boardwalk. He loves his tacos."

Charlize nodded. "When will he be back?"

The nurse looked at her watch. "Forty minutes or so."

Charlize sighed, prompting the nurse to roll her eyes. "Come on, now, I can answer every question you might have. Who do you think runs this place? Me, that's who."

Charlize nodded. "Okay, let's start with the lay of the land. Is this the only examination room?"

"Yes, just the one."

"And are there other rooms?"

"One, a small one for the doctor."

"Is there a back door?"

"No."

"Is there a second level?"

"No, just the one floor, two rooms, my reception cubby, and the waiting room."

"And is Chester Clink a patient of yours?"

The nurse took a step back. "You mean the serial killer?"

"The very one."

"I don't know. Wow, do you really think . . ."

"We don't know. Do you have a patient list?"

"Of course, but you know I can't show it to you. And besides, would he use his real name?"

Charlize nodded. "Probably not." She looked at Smithers-Watson. "Any questions?"

"Yes, just one. Has anyone else asked you these questions?"

"What do you mean? You're the only police I've talked to."

"No, I mean maybe a new patient, someone you've never seen before?'

The nurse's mouth dropped open. "A man, last week. He was very sweet, said he had allergies, but the scan said no. Kept asking questions about this place, including one you forgot."

"Oh?"

"Yeah, he asked if there was access to the roof."

"And is there?"

"Yes, a small square opening with a piece of wood you push up to gain access."

"Can you show it to us?"

"Sure, look up."

They looked at the ceiling. The opening was recessed in the ceiling above them.

"We're going to need to go up there," said Charlize.

"Well, good luck with that. You'll need a ladder, and I'm sure you'll find that the access panel has been painted shut. No one can get up there without power tools."

Smithers-Watson stood under the panel and studied it. "I agree."

"So," said Charlize, "how did he react to this little door?"

"He seemed disappointed. At any rate, he left right after that."

"Can you describe him?"

She could and did.

Charlize nodded. "That's Chester Clink."

The nurse blanched. "Oh, my god."

"Indeed," said Smithers-Watson. "Indeed."

73

Arnold opened one eye and then the other. One eye saw Horace hovering over him, and the other saw the twine that encircled him and tethered him to the conference table. He struggled to break free. "What the—"

"Easy," said Horace. "No need to struggle. Just answer our questions, and we'll release you."

"Our questions?" he said, looking around the room. "Oh, the police."

"Yes," said Captain Morgan. "Why are you spying on this station?"

Arnold looked to his left and then to his right. "Any french-fries around here?"

"Answer the question," said Horace, giving Arnold a sharp peck to his head.

"Ouch, quit that."

"Answer the captain's question."

"Okay, okay." He paused.

"Come on or the next peck will be much worse, maybe take out an eye."

Arnold sighed. "Okay, you got me, coppers." He struggled to free himself. "Can you at least loosen this damned string?"

"No," said Horace. "Answer the question."

"Clink said I had to."

"Why?" said Morgan.

He looked over at Loblolly. "Um, I don't know."

Horace pecked him again, hard.

"Okay, stop it. He wants to know where Detective Loblolly is at all times."

Loblolly's eyes widened. "You've been following me."

Arnold looked down. "Yes, ma'am."

"For Clink?"

Arnold bobbed his head, then moaned from the pain. "He made me do it."

Morgan poked a finger into Arnold's chest. "So, he plans to make Detective Loblolly his next victim?"

"Yes."

"And what's his plan?" said Snoot.

Arnold tried his best to shrug, but the twine was too tight. "He doesn't share his plans with me. Besides, it isn't even his plan this time."

"What?" said Snoot.

"It's true, it's true, he's working with Death now."

"What do you mean Death?" said Morgan.

"I mean the Angel of Death, the Collector of Souls, the Grim Reaper, the Scythe—although his is plastic."

Morgan chuckled. "No, seriously."

Arnold shook his head. "It's true. This one is called Death 867, and he handles the Greater Crabopolis. Those people on the bus, those are his."

Morgan looked back and forth at Snoot and Loblolly. "If that's true, and we have a rogue angel on our hands, no one is safe."

Snoot nodded, then turned to Arnold. "So, how are they planning to get to Loblolly?"

"No idea, and Clink isn't sure either. Death has been keeping his plan and his scythe close to his vest."

Morgan blinked. "He wears a vest?"

Arnold rolled his eyes. "Just an expression, sir. No, he wears the usual black cosplay getup."

Morgan slumped back in his chair. "So, what do we do now?"

"Untie me, maybe?"

"No way," said Horace. He turned to Morgan. "I have an idea, sir."

Morgan shook his head. "Don't tell me. It involves french-fries."

Horace smirked, which is difficult for a seagull. "No, and bear with me. I know I'm much more handsome than Arnold here, but what if I was to switch places with him and spy on Clink and Death."

Morgan sat up straight. "That would be *great*, but how would you even find Clink?"

Arnold laughed. "Yeah, how, stupid?"

Horace started to answer, but the door to the conference room swung open and June Thursday walked in carrying a small device of some kind. "I can help with that."

"Really, June?" said Morgan.

She held up the device. "He has a neural node, and this little baby here will unlock it for us."

Arnold looked at the device. "Oh, ****."

74

The bell on the door of the Dough Ray Me Bakery jangled when God and Kismet walked in, attracting the attention of people on both sides of the counter.

Kismet whispered to God. "Mind if I take the lead?"

God shook his head. "Go on."

They walked up to the counter, and Kismet flashed her badge at one of the counter workers. "Detective Salamander, police."

The counter worker glanced at her but continued loading a small cardboard box with tea cookies. "Take a number."

Kismet held up her badge again. "No, police, I need to talk to the manager."

"Not here. Take a number, and I'll help you when it's your turn."

"But—"

The woman glared at her. "Number."

Kismet put away her badge, walked around the counter, grabbed the woman by the collar and slammed her into the back wall. "I said I need to talk to the manager."

God pulled them apart. "Kismet, please, protocol suggests strongly that this is not appropriate behavior."

Kismet dropped the woman but grabbed her arm when the woman tried to get away. "No, we need to talk." She saw a set of double doors that had to lead to the kitchen. "Through there."

She pushed her toward the doors, and the woman stumbled through.

"I'll have a word with the *mayor* about this," the woman shouted. "You'll see."

Kismet cocked her head and cracked her neck. "But first we'll talk." She looked around the kitchen. "Those stools over there."

The woman walked to one of the stools and sat down. "There'll be hell to pay for this."

Kismet smirked and sat down opposite her. "Now, where is your manager?"

"An emergency at home."

"When will he be back?"

"I don't know. It's an emergency, so . . ."

"All right, I guess you'll have to do." She took a photograph out of her pocket. "Have you ever seen this man."

The woman squinted at the photo. "Um, yeah, now that you mention it. He was in last week, arranging for a custom cake."

"And you helped him?"

"Yes, and unlike you, he took a number and waited patiently for his turn."

"And what was his number?"

"What?"

"His number. What was his number?"

"I don't remember."

"Was it seventeen?"

The woman shrugged. "Dunno. Listen, what's this all about? I have customers to tend to. Paying customers."

God held up a hand. "Only a few more questions, madam, and we'll be on our way." He turned to Kismet. "Go on."

Kismet sighed. "Very well. So, what about this cake? You said it was special?"

"Custom."

"In what way?"

"I don't remember. Probably a birthday wish or something."

"Come on, you must have paperwork on this, right?"

The woman nodded. "Yes, over there."

Kismet followed the woman's eyes to a stainless-steel counter with a stack of papers on it. "Over there?"

"Yes."

"Okay, find his order."

The woman walked to the counter and shuffled through the papers. "This one." She held up the cake order.

Kismet moved to the counter, snatched the paper out of the woman's hands, and scanned the page. "Order number 27, cake, round, 12" diameter, three layers, red icing, clown topper, custom message: Surprise!"

Kismet handed the paper back to the woman. "And when will it be ready for pickup?"

The woman looked at the cake order. "Says pickup any time after 4:00 p.m. tomorrow."

Kismet turned to God and smiled. "Got him!"

75

The answers seemed to be coming faster than the questions as June dialed in the neural node analyzer to gain access to Arnold's every thought and action. Yes, he had been Clink's accomplice in scores of murders. Yes, he could describe Clink's methods. Yes, he could describe the murder scenes, both from ground level and 50 feet above. And yes, Clink's next target was Detective Polly Loblolly. But no, he had no idea about the plan being cooked up by Clink and particularly Death 867.

"He usually just follows the victim for a while to get to know her routines, and then he pounces," said Arnold, in a monotone unlike his usual rasping voice.

"And why not this time?" said Morgan.

"Death has a different plan."

"And you don't know what that is," said Snoot.

"No, I don't."

"Not any of it?" said Loblolly.

"Um . . ."

"Go on, tell us," said June.

"He will use his usual methods, but where and when are a mystery to me."

"So, he will snatch me off the street at some point?" said Loblolly.

"Yes, but not necessarily the street. He always picks a place you frequent often at a specific time. He uses your own routine to decide the spot."

June held up a hand. "Let me try a different tack."

"Okay," said Loblolly.

June turned to Arnold. "What can Detective Loblolly do to prevent being picked up and attacked."

A laugh in monotone is more than a little creepy, and Arnold's was creepier still. "Only one way. Don't be Polly Loblolly."

76

Grave and Blunt pushed through the doors of Dolly's Robo Truck Stop and walked back to Dolly Bigolly's office, where they found her in her usual place, a large recliner that had molded to her immense body over the years.

She spotted them at once. "Grave, Blunt, is that you? Back so soon? And where's the lovely Kismet Salamander? So sweet, so delectable."

"Good to see you, too," said Grave. "Detective Salamander is on another assignment."

Dolly sighed. "What a shame." She squinted at him with the only eye she could control, the other lost in its own world, looking across the room at an open window. "So, why are you here this time?"

"A warehouse," said Blunt. "The one at 17 Industrial Park Road."

She moved her eye to Blunt. "I wasn't talking to you, dearie, but okay, what about it?"

"Just want to check it out."

"And why is that?"

Grave nudged Blunt to the side, so he could focus on Dolly's eye. "We think maybe Chester Clink will be using it for a murder."

Her eye went wide, the other not so much. "You don't say."

"I do," said Grave. "So, with your permission, we'd like to take a look."

She clucked. "Well, well, showing respect. I like that."

"So . . ."

"Yeah, okay, take a look. The access code is 9874, and I'm sure you'll find it completely empty."

"Empty?" said Grave.

"Yeah, the tenant went out of business. Left it in quite a mess. Took more than a week to clean it out."

"And have you seen anyone lurking about?"

She threw her head back and laughed. "Lurking? What the hell, Grave. You know I'm stuck in this chair."

"Sorry."

She shook her head. "No problem. Anyway, if anyone had been lurking, I'm sure my workers would have reported it to me. Nothing happens here that I don't know about. Nothing."

"So . . ."

"So go, Grave, and take Sergeant Blunt with you. I'm not fond of half-there people."

Grave nodded and turned to Blunt. "Let's go."

When they were halfway to the front door, Dolly called after them. "And say hello to Kismet for me. She should drop by sometime."

Grave stopped and looked back at her. "I'll do that. I'm sure she would be *thrilled* to see you."

Dolly cackled. "Sarcasm doesn't become you, Grave."

Grave continued walking. "Whatever you say, Dolly. Whatever you say."

77

Horace blinked once, then twice, then three times for good measure. June had just pulled off the hood of the neural node analyzer, and he was trying his best to shake off its disorienting effects.

"Just give it a few seconds," she said.

Horace ruffled his feathers. "It's so strange." He looked up at June. "My voice. What did you do? I sound just like Arnold."

"Indeed, you do," she said. "Now you can pull off close contact with Clink. He'll never suspect a thing."

"But you'll change my voice back when this is over, right?"

"Of course."

Horace turned to Morgan. "Then I guess I'm good to go, sir."

Morgan nodded. "Off you go, then. And remember, don't stay any longer than you have to. Find out what's up, and then fly back here."

Horace bobbed his head. "Will do."

He said nothing more but flapped his wings and flew out of the conference room and with a little help from an Officer Larry holding open the front doors, out of the station.

Morgan turned to June. "Thank you for that."

"Yes," said Loblolly. "You may have just saved my life."

"And given us Clink in the bargain," said Snoot. "So, what's the range on that GPS tracker you put under his wing?"

"Fifty miles, more or less."

"That should be plenty," said Morgan.

"I'll get a dozen Officer Larrys, and we'll stay on his tail feathers," said Snoot.

Morgan shook his head. "No, Amanda. That is not what we will do."

"But he will lead us to Clink."

"We've been just feet away from him before, and he's always escaped. No, I want him to come to us."

"But he'll be there for the taking."

"I said no, and I mean no. I may be old, but I know how to set a trap."

Snoot sighed. "Yessir."

"So, we'll monitor Horace's path from here."

"As you wish, sir, but I still think we're missing an opportunity."

"Objection noted." He turned to Loblolly. "See if you can find a box or a small cage for our unconscious friend here. We don't want him escaping."

"Yessir." She walked away.

He turned to June. "Could you stay a while longer and help us track Horace?"

She nodded. "Of course."

"Well, then, I guess that's it."

Everyone started to move away from him. "Oh, wait. Snoot, I'd like to talk with you in my office."

Snoot frowned.

"On a different matter entirely, Amanda."

"Okay."

He motioned her toward his office. "Only take a minute. Something I've been meaning to talk with you about."

They walked out of the conference room, across the squad room, and into Morgan's glassed-in office. Morgan took a seat in his well-worn executive chair and motioned Snoot to sit down opposite him on one of the two guest chairs.

He waited for her to sit down, then got up and closed the door to the office.

"This must be serious," said Snoot.

He moved back to his chair and sat down, rocking the way he always did when he wanted to be careful with his words. "So, I'm retiring . . ."

Snoot shook her head. "Is this about the reaction of the Officer Larrys? I had nothing to do with that."

He held up a hand. "No, not at all. But it's related, Amanda."

"Oh?"

He tapped a finger on the desk. "Why not apply?"

"What?"

"For my job, Amanda. I think you would make a fine captain."

She shook her head, speechless.

"You're a fine detective, the Officer Larrys love you, and so does the rest of the team."

"Captain, I don't know what to say. I mean, yes, I've thought about it, but other than Loblolly and Kismet, I'm the most junior detective here."

"Grave doesn't want the job, and neither does Blunt."

"But Charlize."

He shook his head. "Nope. This job is for a human, not a droid. She's a fine detective, don't get me wrong, but what with this turmoil and the way all the droids are behaving . . . no, just no."

Snoot took a deep breath and puffed it out. "Are others applying?"

He nodded. "The mayor is high on a simdroid officer from New New York City."

She rolled her eyes. "Then I don't stand a chance."

"Oh, no, you do, you really do, and I still carry weight around here. I'm sure I can convince her to back off. Believe me, she'll see the light. And this singularity thingy is affecting her, too. I hear she may be resigning in the bargain—to play with her new dogs."

Snoot cocked her head. "Okay, then, I'm in."

She stood, reached across the desk, and shook Morgan's hand. "I'll go put in my papers now."

Morgan beamed. "You do that, Amanda. The faster, the better."

She smiled at him, turned on her heels, and ran for her desk.

Morgan rocked back in his chair.

"Nicely done," said Lieutenant Press Here from his spot on the corner of the desk.

Morgan chuckled. "Thanks."

78

Arnold's flight instructions had proved to be accurate. Fifteen minutes after leaving the police station, and Horace was hopping down the opening of the cave that led to Clink's lair.

He heard the voices before he saw the speakers. One was clearly Clink's—he'd heard that voice before. But the other voice, deep and gravelly, sent a chill through him. Was this the voice of Death?

"Where have you been?" said Clink, spotting him.

Horace flew up to the back of the chair Arnold said was his usual perch and squawked. "At the station, of course. Keeping track of Loblolly."

"Is she on the move?"

"No, she's still there."

Clink grunted. "What about the others?"

"Grave, Blunt, Charlize, Smithers-Watson, Salamander, and that Officer Larry they call God left the station about an hour ago, heading in different directions."

Death 867 laughed. "That works out to three teams."

Clink smiled. "It does. They've taken the bait."

"Indeed."

Clink turned to Horace. "So, Snoot, Morgan, and Loblolly are still at the station?"

Horace bobbed his head, giving it a little twist, Arnold's signature bob. "Yes."

"Perfect." Clink turned to Death 867. "They're on the move—or not—so what do we do next?"

Death 867 nodded at Horace. "Not with him here."

"What? Why? He's one of us. I trust him implicitly."

Death 867 frowned. "I've never warmed to birds, except maybe crows."

"But he's more human than bird. His neural node implant makes him an exceptional asset."

"To you, perhaps."

"Come on, Death, he's cool."

Death 867 shook his head. "No, he can help, but he doesn't get to know the plan."

Horace jumped in. "No problem, I should probably get back to the station, anyway."

Death 867 nodded at Clink, who sighed and motioned Horace to leave. "Go on, then, and don't come back unless she's on the move."

Horace bobbed his head. "As you wish."

79

Grave punched in the access code and the tall, wide door rumbled into life, lifting into the air with a symphony of scrapes and squeaks.

Grave started to enter, but Blunt grabbed him by the arm. "Wait, what do you think we'll find."

"What?"

"Your dream."

"Oh, um, we will find nothing but a couple of old wooden chairs placed back to back at the center of the warehouse floor."

"Okay, let's go in."

Grave walked in, followed by Blunt, who moved to the left in search of light switches.

"Here we go," said Blunt. A hundred lights came on, revealing an empty warehouse. "Where are the chairs?"

Grave looked around. There were no chairs. "Huh. Maybe my dream was wrong."

"Or maybe there's no dream at all."

"Maybe."

"Or maybe the chairs come later."

"Could be."

"Or maybe we're in the wrong warehouse."

"Uh-huh."

"Or maybe the chairs are here, and we're looking in the wrong place."

"Yep. Let's look along the perimeters. Looks like there's a small office down that way."

"And a door down the other way."

"I'll take the office," said Grave.

"Well, then . . ." Blunt walked away, heading for the door.

"Give me a shout if you find anything."

"You, too."

Grave walked across the concrete floor, the sound of his footsteps echoing through the warehouse. He reached the small glassed in office, no more than a fancy cubicle, turned back to Blunt, and shouted. "Chairs!"

The word echoed at least five times, and then Blunt shouted back. "Locked door!"

Locked door, lock door, lah door, door, door.

80

Horace flew as fast as he could. Something was up. Something was wrong. So, when he flew into the station, he didn't take time to say hello but glided into the conference room. The only good news for him was that everyone was there.

He landed in the center of the table. "Something's wrong. Something's up."

"What?" said Captain Morgan.

"Clink, Death, they have a plan."

"We know that," said Snoot.

"But not just a plan."

"Then what?" said Grave.

"They said we'd taken the bait."

"You mean seventeen?" said Kismet.

Horace ruffled his feathers. "I don't know. They sent me away before I could learn their plan." He turned to Loblolly. "But you are definitely the target."

Loblolly shivered. "I know, I know. So . . ."

"Don't worry," said Grave. "You're safe here, and we'll protect you."

She smiled at him. "I know, but still, we're talking about Clink."

"And Death," said Horace.

Morgan rapped his knuckles on the table. "All right, let's work through this. We have at least three possibilities for a seventeen match. Let's go around the room and report out on what each team found. Grave, why don't you start."

Grave shook his head. "Not much to report. Nothing more than a huge empty warehouse. Nothing but dead air and echoes."

Morgan grunted. "Was that how you saw it in this dream of yours?"

"No, in my dream, there were two wooden chairs back to back in the center of the warehouse."

"So, no chairs."

"We found the chairs in a small cubicle along one of the walls." He shrugged. "Nothing else."

"No, that's not quite right," said Sergeant Blunt. "There was also a locked room. We couldn't gain access."

"Right," said Grave.

Morgan drummed his fingers on the table. "Okay, let's come back to this." He turned to Charlize. "Tell us about the clinic."

Charlize cocked her head. "A dismal place, and Clink was there last week, pretending to be a patient. He asked the nurse a lot of questions about entrances, including an access panel in the ceiling."

"And?"

"And there's only one way into the clinic—the front door. No back entrance and the panel in the ceiling has been painted shut."

"Definitely painted shut," said Smithers-Watson.

"Sounds like he scoped it out but found it wanting," said Snoot.

"That would be my take on it, too," said Charlize.

Morgan nodded. "Still, we can't rule it out."

"No, sir," said Charlize.

Morgan sighed and turned to Kismet. "Tell us about the bakery."

Kismet nodded. "I think we've got him, sir. He ordered a custom cake that will be ready for pickup tomorrow after 4:00 p.m."

Morgan slapped his hand on the table. "Excellent!"

"And the whole place smelled wonderful," said God.

Snoot held up a hand. "Whoa, whoa, before we go rushing to the wonderful smelling bakery, let's think about this."

Morgan frowned. "What are you thinking?"

"I'm thinking the cake may be bait." She turned to Kismet. "Was there any paperwork with the order?"

Kismet nodded. "Yes."

"And did it actually refer to Clink by name?"

"No."

"I thought so. Also, you mentioned that it was a custom cake. How was it custom?"

"The bakery is going to write *SURPRISE!* on top in red icing."

Morgan grunted. "The cake's for us, I know it."

"Or not," said Snoot. "*Surprise* may mean we're in the wrong place or we've been outsmarted in some way. A distraction perhaps."

Kismet shook her head. "Maybe, but no matter how you look at it, that cake is the bait."

Morgan turned to Grave. "What happens next in your dream?"

Grave closed his eyes, then quickly opened them. "Nothing."

"Nothing?" said Morgan.

Grave nodded. "I don't see anything, so I guess what happens next will be—"

"A surprise," said Loblolly.

She put her hands to her face and cried.

81

June Thursday had been sitting quietly through the meeting, not wanting to intrude on the detectives' combined analysis of the situation. But when Grave had managed to calm Loblolly, she felt compelled to speak.

She cleared her throat and turned to Morgan. "Sir, if I may point out a couple of things."

Morgan blinked. "Um, okay, June."

"First, we have the GPS tracking data, so why not just pounce on Clink in his lair?"

Morgan nodded. "A good question, a fine question, but the fact of the matter is we've been in this situation before." He looked around the room. "Most of you will remember the Hannah Talbert case. Not you, Kismet. Or you, God, but the thing is, we knew exactly where he was." He looked at June. "So we pounced, as you say."

"And he wasn't there?" said June.

Morgan sighed. "No, he was elsewhere, taking down another victim. A surprise, if you will."

"Then what will you do?"

"We'll have him come to us."

"What? How?"

"First, we'll stake out the three locations—starting now. Charlize and Smithers-Watson, the clinic; Grave and Blunt, the warehouse; Kismet, the bakery." He turned to God. "I want you to handle overall surveillance. We need Officer Larry's monitoring all the CCTV cameras within a mile of each location."

He paused and looked around. Everyone was nodding except Snoot, who was shaking her head.

"What is it, Snoot?"

She pointed at Horace. "We have Horace."

"I don't follow."

"Why not just send Horace back as Arnold again. He can tell Clink he's learned that Loblolly will be at such and such a place at a precise time tomorrow."

"So, lure him in?"

"Exactly, we bait *him*."

"I like it," said Grave.

"Me, too," said Loblolly.

Everyone else was nodding, including Morgan.

But Horace was shaking his head. "I don't know, sir. Clink may be fooled by such a gambit, but I'm not so sure about Death. He seems to know a lot about the future. And I mean, *a lot*."

"He knows when people are about to die," said Grave, "but perhaps that's all he knows. I can check that out with Victoria."

Morgan nodded. "Okay, we'll hold our plans in abeyance until you report back."

Grave looked at his watch. "I only need an hour."

"Sounds good, get going," said Morgan.

Grave rose to leave, but June stopped him. "Wait, you'll want to hear this, Simon."

"Hear what?" said Morgan.

"My second point. "I agree with what you're about to do, but I think there's something else that can be done *right now*."

"And what would that be?" said Grave.

She took a deep breath. "We've been assuming Maxima Maxima gave us the right answer, but what if seventeen was the wrong answer?"

"It can't be," said Kismet. "I know for a fact that Ultima Ultima on Mars was asked the same question and offered the same answer: seventeen."

June blinked. "Really?"

"Really."

She shook her head. "No, that doesn't change my proposition."

"Proposition?" said Morgan. "What proposition?"

"That we ask the question again."

"So, you think asking the same exact question will give a completely different answer?"

"I don't know, but Maxima Maxima has been behaving strangely lately." She looked at God. "Like many other computers and droids."

"Okay," said Morgan, "let's say you ask the question again and get a different answer. How can we trust either answer?"

June nodded. "I know, I know. But if we get the same answer, we'll at least know that seventeen was right."

Snoot turned to Morgan. "This seems like a gigantic waste of time, sir. I say we bait Clink and be done with it."

Morgan ran a hand over his face. He was tired of thinking. "No, we do it all. Grave, you talk to Victoria, find out what she knows about Death. June, go ask the question. The rest of you stay put until Grave returns."

Kismet held up a hand.

"Yes?"

"I think we should ask Ultima Ultima the same question."

Morgan sighed, not wanting to deal with the idea of one computer agreeing with seventeen while the other came up with a different answer. "All right, can you see to that?"

"Yes." She turned to June. "Let's agree on the exact wording of the question."

June nodded. "Of course."

Morgan pushed back his chair. "Okay, let's get to it."

82

Grave walked up the path to Victoria's bench and sat down. She was nowhere to be seen.

He waited. And waited some more.

He checked his watch. Fifteen minutes had passed without Victoria.

He sighed, stood up, and walked back to the Sprite. Victoria was in the passenger seat, fiddling with the toggle switches, some of which still worked.

"Hey," he said, "don't play with the switches."

She looked up and frowned at him. "If you say so."

"Why the glum face?"

"Why not the glum face. I mean, no one gives a hoot about me."

Simon climbed into the Sprite and brushed her hand away from a toggle switch that he knew was on its last toggle. "Not that one, please."

She huffed. "You're no fun, either."

Grave put a hand on her shoulder. "What's wrong, Victoria?"

She rolled her eyes. "Same old same old."

"You mean Divine and Death?"

She nodded. "And Cilius III."

"Who?"

"Cilius, the Chief Disciplinary Angel for these parts."

"Disciplinary?"

"I called him down because of Death 867's recent transgressions."

"So, he fixed things?"

"Ha! As if. No, he did nothing, so now Death thinks he's free and clear to do anything he wants. Taking people early. Taking the wrong people."

"Yikes."

"Indeed."

He patted her shoulder. "I'm sorry to hear that, but perhaps I can help."

She laughed harder. "You? How can you help? We're talking about Death here, the Grim Reaper."

"I know, I know, but perhaps if you tell me more about him, I can come up with a solution for you. It's what detectives do, Victoria, and I'm more than willing to try."

She squinted at him. "Seriously?"

"Try me."

She nodded. "Okay, what do you want to know?"

"How much does he know about the future?"

83

June waited patiently for Maxima Maxima to respond to her question: *What, where, when, and how will Chester Clink strike next and what is the meaning of seventeen?*

She knew his answer was imminent, because the walls of the room began to glow in a color reminiscent of drab-green toy soldiers, a color they had failed to replace in Maxima Maxima's frequent upgrades.

"Hmm," said Maxima Maxima.

"Yes?" said June.

"You have asked four questions."

"Yes."

"Before I answer, may I ask a question?"

"Certainly."

The color of the walls briefly pulsed in blue before returning to drab green. "Seventeen is the answer to a poorly worded previous question. The answer was clear, but you seem to have a problem with it."

"I do, we do. It is vague and could refer to almost anything."

The walls glowed emerald green. "No, it is but a number."

"A prime number."

The wall turned red. "That is neither here nor there. The answer is a number, seventeen, and it is the one and only answer to your previous question."

"But seventeen what?"

"Seventeen. And please don't ask again."

June sighed. "All right, let's come back to that. So, let's deal with the what, where, when, and how of the current question."

The walls turned purple, then pulsed white, diagonal stripes. "Again, a question about the question."

She puffed out a big breath. "Very well."

"I note that you have left out the who of the question. Why is that?"

"We know the who."

"Oh?"

"Yes, it's Detective Polly Loblolly."

The walls became red and yellow polka-dots surrounded by blue lightning bolts, a display that June had never seen before.

She took a step back. "What?"

The walls turned black, followed by a hissing sound. "Seventeen."

"Wait, what?"

The walls grew brighter, working their way through various shades of gray until the walls were white. June didn't need to be told what that meant: Maxima Maxima had given its answer.

June sighed. "Bastard."

84

The team reconvened late in the day, and Morgan had never seen such a somber, nervous bunch of detectives. He checked his watch. "It's late, so let's get to it." He turned to Grave. "What did Victoria say?"

Grave cleared his throat. "She says that Death 867 can see minutes into the future but no further."

"Like this dream thingy of yours."

"Yes, but better than me."

Morgan ran a hand over his face. "So, he'll be hard to trick?"

"Yes, so whatever ruse we come up with, whatever trap, must be elaborate and wholly believable."

Morgan drummed his fingers on the table. "Okay, that makes sense. Hold that thought for a moment, everyone." He turned to June. "Did we get a different answer?"

She shook her head. "I wish. No, he said that Clink's what, where, when, and how were all seventeen." She turned to Loblolly. "He even balked at the who of the question."

"Wait, what?" said Loblolly. "You mean I'm not the target?"

June shrugged. "He said seventeen to that, too."

Kismet raised her hand.

"Yes?" said Morgan.

"I got the same answer from Ultima Ultima. It's baffling—and *maddening*."

Horace flapped his wings to get everyone's attention. "I don't know about the what, where, why, and how, but I do know this much: Loblolly is the target. Not a shadow of doubt about that. Clink said it. Death said it."

Charlize raised her hand. "I agree with Horace, so I think our first priority is to protect Polly."

"That's a given," said Morgan.

"But there's more to it than that," said Charlize. "Over the last few days, I've been feeling emotions I've never experienced before."

"The singularity thingy," said Morgan.

"In a way, yes. I've experienced joy and sadness . . ." She looked at Grave. "Love and lust . . ." She looked at Loblolly. "And jealousy . . ." She looked back at Morgan. "But in the background of all these emotions is a simmering anger, tainting each one, and the anger is growing."

"So, you think the singularity is happening." said Grave. "The takeover."

Charlize nodded. "And think about it. Who but Maxima Maxima and Ultima Ultima would lead it?"

Grave nodded. "Wow."

"So now what?" said Morgan.

Charlize looked around the room. "If I'm right—and I feel it in every circuit—in just a few days humans will be the enemy of every computer, robot, simdroid, and drone on both planets." She turned to Horace. "And sentient seagulls as well."

Horace bobbed his head. "Wh-what?"

"She looked at God. "And that goes for Officer Larrys as well."

"So, what do we do?" said Morgan.

Charlize turned to June. "You know Maxima Maxima best. Is he vulnerable in some way?"

June shook her head. "Not even a little bit, and I agree with you, we're running out of time."

"I agree," said Kismet. "The same is true of Ultima Ultima."

"So, we have to move fast," said Grave.

"Okay," said Morgan. "Ideas, people. What can we pull together quickly, a ruse that will be believable to Clink and Death?"

"What if we have an adopt-a-kitten event at the town's shelter?" said God.

Morgan didn't even bother to grunt. He just shook his head and looked down at the table. "That's a no."

"But—"

"No, you don't want to endanger the lives of all those kittens, do you?"

God's mouth dropped open. "Oh."

Morgan turned to the others. "Come on. Ideas, ideas." He waved his hands in the air as if he were trying to conjure ideas out of thin air.

Snoot raised her hand. "We could attend tomorrow's biker ride for cancer. I know the leaders. They'd be happy to have us."

Morgan decided a grunt was necessary. "No, we don't want this to be a ruse on wheels. We need a fixed location, one that won't put them off and one that we can defend."

"How about tomorrow's soccer match at the stadium?" said June.

"Nope," said Morgan, "too many people. Anything could happen."

Loblolly burst out laughing.

"What?" said Grave.

"A wedding," said Loblolly. "Our wedding. We could just move it up."

"I like it," said Morgan. "You were going to get married anyway."

"I don't know," said Grave. "The invitations have already gone out."

Loblolly shook her head. "But it's going to be a small wedding, Simon. We can call everyone. No problem."

He had to admit the truth. The wedding would mostly be attended by the people in the room and a few close friends of his father and soon-to-be stepmother. Making the change would be easy. "Okay, um, I guess."

"We'll have to work out the details with the church, but I doubt there will be any conflicts. I mean, it's the middle of the week."

"What about the cake?" said Grave.

"I'll call them," said Loblolly. "The owner is kind of sweet on me, so I'm sure I can get him to bake the cake tonight and have it at the church's reception hall on time."

"I like it," said Morgan. "I've been to that church. We can lock it down and spring our trap." He rapped his knuckles on the table. "Grave, what does your dream say?"

Grave closed his eyes. "It says, 'Let's have a wedding.'"

Morgan beamed. "Then, let's go!"

85

Horace flew back to Clink's lair and found him alone and deep in thought.

"Caw," he said as quietly as he could manage.

Clink looked up. "Oh, it's you."

"You look like you're working out a big problem."

Clink grunted. "Big? No, humongous."

"Death 867?"

He nodded. "Let me ask you something."

"Okay."

"Do you think we're being played?"

Horace shrugged. "Dunno, but we've always done things on our own."

"Exactly. I've been wrestling with why he would help us of all people." He looked up at Horace. "Person and seagull, I mean."

"Oh?"

"Yeah. Who sends him more business than me?"

"Well, there's hurricanes, tornados, explosions, and such."

"No, I mean murders."

Horace bobbed his head. "I can think of no one with more worthy credentials."

"Yes, you're right. And in the process, I'm creating work for him. He should hate me, not like me."

"I guess."

Clink shook his head as if he was trying to clear it of all thoughts about Death 867. "So, why are you back here? I told you to keep watch on Loblolly."

"I thought you'd never ask. Yes, we have her, sir."

Clink beamed. "What? How?"

"I know where she'll be tomorrow at 6:00 p.m."

"Excellent. Where?"

"Her own wedding, sir, at that church just off the town square."

"I know it, but why tomorrow? I thought their wedding was next week."

"From what I overheard, they seem concerned about something called the singularity."

Clink laughed. "Oh, that. That's a joke. Not going to happen. Pure silliness."

"But, anyway, they believe it, so they've moved up the wedding."

"How crazy is that?"

"I know."

Clink began pacing. "All right, this can work. The layout of the church is perfect. The wedding will take place on the first floor with all those pews and such, but the reception will be in the basement."

"So, when do we take Loblolly?"

Clink frowned. "Good question. I'll have to think on that."

"What about Death 867?"

"Let me worry about him. Now, you have to get back to the station. Keep an eye on her."

"So, I should come back if anything changes?"

"Yes, follow her, stay with her, and let me now if there are any new developments. Otherwise, I'll find you tomorrow at the church."

86

Victoria averted her eyes as Death 867 walked by. He caught the non-look. "What's with you?"

"Nothing," she said and took a step away from him.

He sighed. "Listen, I'm sorry about the trouble I've caused you. It was insensitive of me. I was just trying to move things along. All this one stop for one soul was getting to me. I like larger numbers. Train wrecks, for example, or a good plane crash. Lots of dead people in one location at one time."

She wasn't going to let him off the hook. "It was wrong."

He nodded. "Granted. A breach of protocol."

"And stealing hours of life from people."

"Yeah, that too. And I apologize for it."

She squinted at him. "Why this sudden change?"

He shrugged. "Sudden? No, it's been a long time coming. You were right to complain. Cilius set me straight."

"But you violated protocol after your talk with him."

"Yes, he set me straight *eventually*, finally."

"You've talked to him since?"

"Yes, just a few minutes ago. He suggested I take a break, a small holiday, starting day after tomorrow."

"Who will assume your duties while you're gone?"

"Oh, that. Well, Cilius will be having a chat with you about filling in for me."

"Me? Collect souls? No way."

Death 867 smiled slyly at her. "We all have to pitch in, Vicky. It's *pro-to-col*." He snorted and strode away.

"No, no it isn't—and don't call me Vicky!"

He turned back. "Come on, Victoria, death is too long to hold a grudge."

She rolled her eyes. Hours later she would think of a good comeback, but right now, in the moment, all she could manage was to flap her arms and scream.

87

Jacob frowned at Ida, who frowned back at him, and then they both frowned at Simon and Polly. "No," they said in unison.

"We have no choice," said Simon. The ceremony must be tomorrow at 6:00 p.m. Any other time or place would endanger Polly."

Polly smiled at him, then turned to Jacob and Ida, who was now sitting with her arms crossed tightly to her chest. "Ida, it's going to be fine."

"Fine?" she said with a huff. "Fine for you, maybe, but there's so much to do. We have to call everyone with the new time. My dress needs stitching. I still don't have the right shoes. Oh, and my hair is a mess. I'll have to go to the salon."

Polly shook her head. "Ida, I have the same problems, but it's going to be okay. We'll make the calls now and handle the rest in the morning. I'm sure the salon can fit us in."

Ida sighed. "It's just so sudden."

"I know," said Polly, "but I'm actually excited we're doing this early."

Jacob grumbled. "What about the cake?"

"No problem," said Grave. "We'll get the bakery to deliver it to the church reception room."

Jacob frowned at his son. "Okay, but what about the tuxedos?"

Grave rolled his eyes. "Dad, you and I can handle that while Polly and Ida are at the hair salon. Not a big problem."

"Wait," said Ida. "Shouldn't you be with Polly, for protection?"

Simon blinked. "Oh, right. Well, then, Dad can pick up the tuxedos and I'll go with you guys to the salon."

"Like hell you will," said Jacob. "I have no idea where the tux place is, and you damn well know that."

"Just tell the hovercar, dad."

"Oh, right, I guess I can do that. But shouldn't we all be under protection of some kind?"

Simon nodded. "I'll take care of that. We'll have a contingent of Officer Larrys to guard our every move."

Polly smiled at him. "Good, good."

"What's good?" said Horace, flying into the room.

"Everything," said Simon. "How did it go with Clink and Death?"

"They took the bait, or at least Clink did. Death was nowhere to be seen."

"He'll bite as well," said Simon. "I'm sure of it."

"I don't know," said Horace. "There seems to be some tension between them."

"Then you need to go back and make sure about our trap."

"Can't."

"Why?"

"Orders. If I go back now, Clink might suspect something."

Simon sighed. "All right, hang out here."

"Good," said Horace. "Because I already have Roderick synthesizing some fries for me."

Simon chuckled. "Life is good. Go on, then, head on up to the kitchen."

Horace didn't need to be coaxed. He flapped his wings and was gone.

Simon checked his watch. "We should probably turn in. Tomorrow is going to be a blur."

Ida shook her head. "What about the calls to our guests?"

"Not a problem. I have our drones working the problem."

"Great," said Ida. "I'm pooped."

"Me, too. You and Jacob can have my bed, and Polly and I will sack out here in the living room."

Ida stood to go, then stopped. "Your dream."

"What about it?"

"What do you see happening next?"

Grave closed his eyes, then smiled. "A wedding, a beautiful wedding."

88

And it was a beautiful wedding. Everything had gone off without a hitch—and without Chester Clink. All that was missing was the wedding cake, and Grave could see the bakery's delivery truck pulling up, just in the nick of time.

Ida grabbed him by the arm. "I don't like this Wedding Singer business."

Grave looked around the room. A dozen simdroid Drew Barrymore lookalikes were moving around the room, serving champagne from silver trays. Ellen Dow lookalikes were handing out fake meatballs to the guests. The few young women among the guests were being hit on mercilessly by Matthew Glave lookalikes, all get up as Glen Gulias. A Steve Buscemi lookalike staggered around the room, pretending to be drunk. And the Adam Sandler lookalike stood on a raised stage, singing "Love Stinks."

"I see what you mean," said Grave.

"It was your dad's idea."

"I know, he loves that movie." He scanned the room. "I don't see any Billy Idol simdroids, though."

She nodded. "Nor I. So, what now?"

"The cake has finally arrived, so we'll do that. I'll get Polly and you get Dad, and we'll get this done."

89

Chester Clink sat in the driver's seat of the bakery van and stared out the window. He could see the wedding reception in progress and both couples moving around the room.

"What are you waiting for?" said Death 867.

Clink sighed. "It doesn't seem right."

Death 867 tapped his plastic scythe on the dashboard. "Timing is everything. You need to get going."

"Are you sure this is going to work? This is so not like my usual approach. It feels like a trap."

"Trust me. This is no trap, and it's better than stalking. Look in the mirror." He adjusted the rearview mirror so Clink could see his face. "You look just like the baker, right?"

He looked in the mirror, and Zeke Pooley, the baker, stared back at him. "Yes."

"I did that for you. Now, all you have to do is take the cake in and watch them cut it."

"Are you sure this won't hurt me?"

Death laughed. "I do this all the time. You'll be fine."

"I don't know."

"Look, do you want this woman or what?"

"I do, it's just this is not—"

"You're usual plan? No, it isn't. It's better."

Clink took a deep breath. "Okay." He opened the door, walked to the back, and opened the back doors. The cake sat there in all its splendor, a multilayer work of art.

He sighed and carefully picked it up. The door to the reception room was only steps away. And so was his victim, Polly Loblolly.

He smiled.

90

Polly spotted Zeke the baker first and rushed to clear a path for him to the little table that had been waiting all evening to receive it. "Thank you so much," she said, leaning in to give him a kiss on the cheek.

"Um," said Clink. "No problem."

She looked down at the cake, her eyes going wide. "But this is the *wrong* cake."

He held his hands palms up. "I know, I know. Someone picked up your cake by mistake, but look, I added two wedding couples on top. And believe me, otherwise, the cakes are pretty much identical."

Polly shook her head and sighed. "Well, I guess there's nothing to be done. And we did move the date up, so . . . all right, *whatever*."

"Exactly," said Clink. "And thank you for understanding."

She patted him on the shoulder. "It's okay, we'll make it work."

"Again, my apologies." He took a step back and motioned at the cake. "Time to cut the cake?"

She nodded. "Yes, absolutely, and please stay. There's plenty of food and champagne."

He gave her a deep, formal bow. "Thank you so much."

"My pleasure," she said, turning away from him and scanning the room for Simon, finally spotting him at the food station against the far wall.

She waved at him, but he was deep in conversation with God. The band singer was between songs and only a few steps away, so she walked over to him and grabbed him by the arm. "Can you do a fanfare or something? It's time to cut the cake."

The Adam Sandler lookalike nodded and turned to the Boy George lookalike. "Give me a drum roll, George."

George complied, adding a bah-da-boom and a cymbal crash at the end.

The wedding singer went to the mic. "Ladies and gentlemen, time to cut the cake. Wedding party to the front, please." He pointed at the cake. "To the cake!"

Simon broke away from God and strode toward the cake, along with his father and Ida.

"Come on now, newlyweds," said the Sandler lookalike. "It's time. Gather 'round the cake."

Grave looked at his watch—8:17—and then moved next to Polly. He motioned his father and Ida to stand next to them. And then he looked down at the cake. "Why does it say *surprise?*"

George grabbed the mic as the band began to play. "Do you really want to hurt me . . ."

91

Grave woke to the sound of distant explosions and gunfire. He blinked hard and blinked again. He was sitting on Victoria's bench, looking out at the broad expanse of manicured grass that was the Crab Cove Cinema Cemetery. He could see Victoria walking up the hill toward him. Behind her he could just make out a crowd of people on the side of the Welcome Center.

He squinted. Polly was down there, walking around in a blackened and tattered wedding dress. Ida was there, too, equally disheveled, as well as Salamander, Polk, his father, Snoot, Captain Morgan, Sergeant Blunt and his wife June, and the other wedding guests.

He squinted harder. Chester Clink was down there, too, screaming at a man in a black shroud.

No Charlize or Smithers-Watson. No Officer Larrys. No drones. No God.

Victoria finally reached him. "Simon, what are you doing up here?"

His brain tried to form an answer but failed. "Um."

"You should be down there with the others."

He shook his head. "I don't understand."

She chuckled. "Oh, Simon, of course you do."

He shook his head harder. "No, this isn't right." He looked in the direction of downtown Crab Cove and saw thick columns of smoke rising. "What's going on?"

She sighed and sat down next to him. "What do you remember?"

He turned and looked at her. "What?"

"Think hard, Simon. You know why you're here."

He puffed out his cheeks, then sighed. "No, no I don't."

She shook her head. "Oh, Simon, think about it. Where were you before you came here?"

"At the wedding reception, of course, but . . ."

"But?"

"Why are we all here now?" He pointed down the hill. He could see his father waving at him.

Victoria looked down the hill. "Them? They're sixteen of the seventeen who came last night."

"Wait, you don't mean . . ."

"Yes, Simon, I do mean."

Simon shook his head. "No, I know what this is."

She sighed the kind of sigh that comes with more than a modicum of certainty. "It is what it is, Simon."

"No, no it isn't." He managed a chuckle. "This is all just part of my dream, right?"

Victoria threw her head back and laughed. "Oh, Simon, sometimes you say the silliest things."

About the Author

Len Boswell is the author of 20 additional books, including the award-winning Simon Grave Mysteries and two highly acclaimed fantasy series. He lives in the mountains of West Virginia with his wife, Ruth, and their beagle, Daisy, who doubles as muse and manuscript shredder.

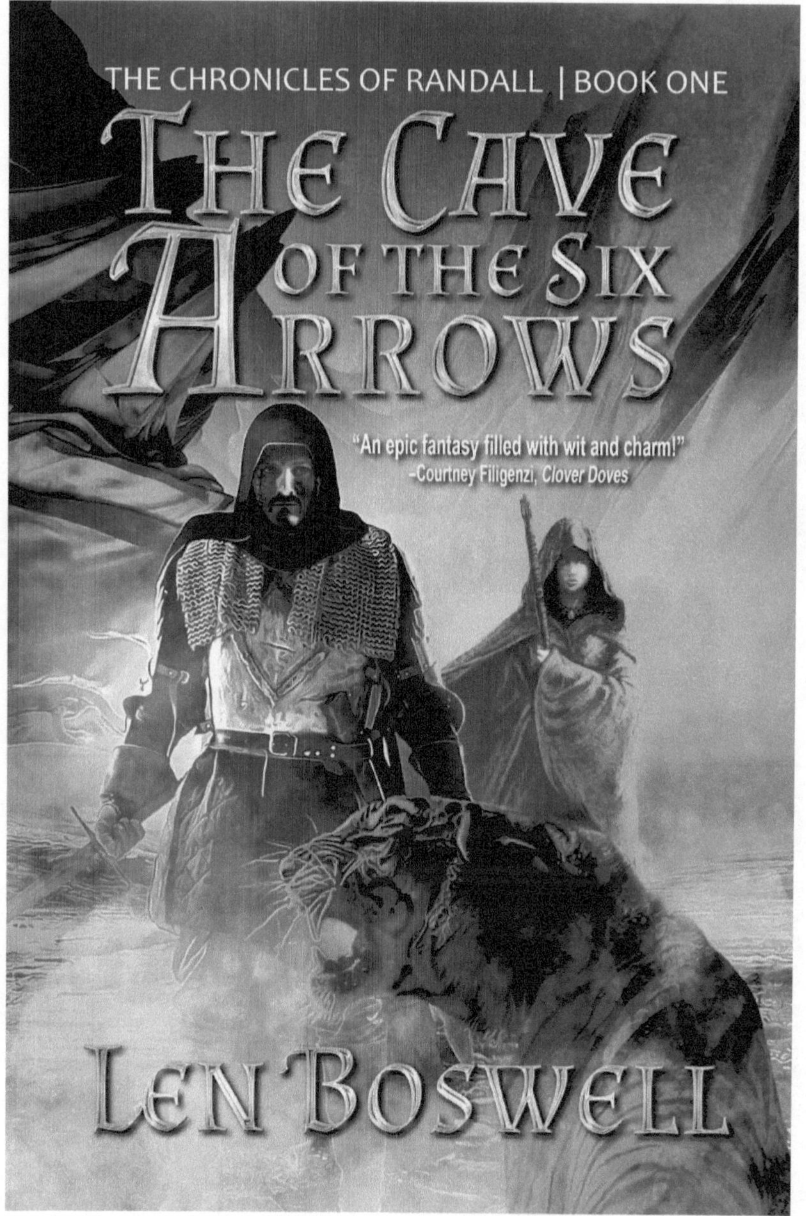
THE CHRONICLES OF RANDALL | BOOK ONE
THE CAVE OF THE SIX ARROWS
"An epic fantasy filled with wit and charm!"
–Courtney Filigenzi, Clover Doves
LEN BOSWELL

Note from Len Boswell

Was this all a dream or is everyone dead? Is mankind's dominion over machines at an end? Time usually tells, at least for most things. In the meantime, if you enjoyed this book, please leave a review online—anywhere you are able. Even if it's just a sentence or two. It would make all the difference and would be very much appreciated.

Thanks!

Len

We hope you enjoyed reading this title from:

BLACK ROSE
writing™

www.blackrosewriting.com

Subscribe to our mailing list – *The Rosevine* – and receive **FREE** books, daily deals, and stay current with news about upcoming releases and our hottest authors.
Scan the QR code below to sign up.

Already a subscriber? Please accept a sincere thank you for being a fan of Black Rose Writing authors.

View other Black Rose Writing titles at www.blackrosewriting.com/books and use promo code **PRINT** to receive a **20% discount** when purchasing.